NO ONE TO HOLD THE DISTANT DEAD

K.L. Schroeder

PSYCHOPOMP

FOR THE FREJ/AS
OF THIS WORLD.
————

NO ONE TO HOLD THE DISTANT DEAD

© 2025 K.L. Schroeder
All Rights Reserved.

ISBN-13: 979-8-89116-017-0

Published by Psychopomp
psychopomp.com

Publisher's Note:
No part of this publication may be reproduced, distributed, or transmitted in any form or by any means, including photocopying, recording, or other electronic or mechanical methods, without the prior written permission of the publisher, except in the case of brief quotations embodied in critical reviews and certain other noncommercial uses permitted by copyright law.

This book is a work of fiction. Names, characters, places, and incidents either are products of the author's imagination or are used fictitiously. Any resemblance to actual persons, living or dead, events, or locales is entirely coincidental.

Cataloging-in-Publication Data
Names: Schroeder, K.L., author.
Title: No One to Hold the Distant Dead
Description: Woodbury, VT : Psychopomp [2025]
Identifiers: ISBN: 9798891160170 (paperback)
Subjects: LCSH: Science fiction. |
BISAC: FICTION / Science fiction / General. |

Cover & interior formatted by Christine M. Scott
clevercrow.com

Cover illustration "Body Transfer" by MMIX
(Rust MacCarthy & L Faunt)

AUTHOR'S NOTE

This is a story about death,
and what we do when faced with an end.
In it there are deaths of people and of wildlife.
I am faithful to the gravity of their loss.
Take care of yourself while reading.

TABLE OF CONTENTS

CHAPTER 1 1

CHAPTER 2 5

CHAPTER 3 13

CHAPTER 4 21

CHAPTER 5 33

CHAPTER 6 45

CHAPTER 7 53

CHAPTER 8 61

CHAPTER 9 69

CHAPTER 10 79

CHAPTER 11 85

CHAPTER 12 93

CHAPTER 13 97

1

Everyone had talked about space travel as rebirth. My journey was a death.

The first of many.

Beaming my consciousness all the way to Nordenmark took an entire Earth year, little waves of memory and personality floating through the vacuum of space—how formaldehyde was sweet in my nose, the cold sand of the Canadian desert crunching between my teeth, the motion of my hand drawing thick black lines over my eyelids every morning. I extruded out through the void and for a year collected in a storage device in the Godhavn medical station, a hundred light-years away, somewhere beside a pinprick of light in Earth's night sky. People spoke about it with reverence; it would be like coming out of a warm darkness, the womb of time itself, taking a first breath of another planet's air like an infant, a new body soft and unspoiled. How lucky I was.

It was nothing like that.

I came to on an operating table screaming, struggling to breathe through a searing pain in my chest, to see through a blinding light.

"She's back. Looks stable."

"You're okay Inga, deep breaths, you're alright."

The unfamiliar proportions of the new body made rolling over difficult. Hips that had none of their previous weight, ribs that shrank around shallow lungs. A hand pressed on one of my new shoulders, the bones protruding and small. A woman with thin blonde hair trimmed in a short fringe bent next to me.

"My chest..." I whispered.

"I know. We had to depolarize you, there was a problem with the waking routine once you were all here. You'll be alright in a few minutes—give her some recovery media, Kristoffer."

Coolness crept up one of my arms, dulling the pain. Her worried face gave a brief smile, lighting her catlike eyes. "Welcome to Nordenmark, Inga. We are so glad you are finally here. I'm Eva, this is Kristoffer. We communicated with you last year, before you started beaming in."

My breath caught on the pain in my side as I started to push myself up. I had expected the blue circle of light leaking through the skin over my collarbone, but not the rest of the changes. "Why is this body...it's...so different."

The two exchanged a look.

"There should be an update in your memory cores on what's been happening here." I felt the leads tug as Kristoffer fiddled with a monitor hooked into one of the weedy wrists. "You should be able to remember."

Deep breaths. As much air as I could hold. "Remember what?"

Another look. Eva began tapping on a computer terminal next to me. "Vitals are normal. You don't remember anything from the last year?"

"Nothing after leaving Earth." The tiny frame, this new skeleton, felt too fragile to withstand the pain. I wrapped the arms around myself, tried to comfort it. Me. "I was in the preparation lab in Edmonton. There was a technician there with me, he said to say hello…" A shooting pain in my temple cut the words off. No, there hadn't been a technician, I'd been alone in the preparation lab. Or someone was missing. There was some kind of absence, but I didn't remember what. A whimper escaped. "There's nothing else. What did I miss?"

"Well, the ecologists are saying it's the end of—"

Eva cut him off. "The situation has gotten worse. The synthesis labs are trying to keep pace with accelerating foodstock loss, so their facilities are overworked." Kristoffer crossed his arms over his chest as she continued. "The priority was to finish printing the organic matrix for your brain, which they just finished in time, so the rest of you is a little…underdeveloped."

"What does that mean." The room swam, and I rubbed my hand over the back of my neck, fingers meeting long hair. That wasn't how I had left it either. "Gods, I'm dizzy. Is that normal?"

"I'm not sure." My eyes tried to catch Kristoffer's floating voice. "The protocol says you should rest for four hours and then start with daily routines."

"That probably doesn't account for being depolarized," Eva grumbled from somewhere behind me. My eyes began to beat to the side, like I had been spinning for hours.

There had only been twelve people beamed to other planets before me, and I was the first to Nordenmark. I had known the risk. Bringing Earth's knowledge to a community in crisis was a huge honour. I shook my head to try and resolve the room around me, arm twisting as I fell against the bed. Hands pulled my limbs gently to rest as the blood in my ears drowned out Eva and Kristoffer's urgent voices.

The abyss that leapt to envelop me was cold, roaring yet horribly still.

2

It took two days to stabilize my brain inside my new body. Two days until I could stand alone at the mirror, cutting the hair of the reflected stranger so that it brushed my jaw like it had on Earth. Even then, a cold shadow clung as I walked out of the medical station, like the wisps of white fog that hung in low areas of the dim streets, swirling around passersby like little forked tongues. They lapped at my ankles as I passed through the gates of the medical station into the flat light of a city swarmed over with dark green vegetation.

Godhavn itself didn't look much different from the reels I'd watched on Earth a year ago: low stone and wood buildings lit by a distant, pale star. The air was thick with humidity, and the buzz of slow-moving drones mingled with thuds of heavy machinery. But the people who walked by me, their dull eyes passing over the weeds that burst through the street, their movements dazed and slow, they were different. They showed the weight of the past year, of Nordenmark's precipitous fall into full-blown ecological collapse.

The digital assistant in the bracelet wearable Eva had given me directed me to a store marked with a crooked green cross. The building was coated in grime, containers of tomatoes and insect flour ghostly through the oily windows. Inside, open baskets were heaped with bundles of vegetables—shoots and dark leaves and bulbs from silver to dark purple—but in the dusty aisles beyond, cans and boxes of synthetic nutrient pastes were strewn across near-empty shelves. A heavy older man sat behind a counter, fingers tapping a mobile terminal that rested against his stomach. He glanced up at me from the small screen where a young avatar with brilliant blue hair worked in a zoo of vibrant animals. I gave him a nod of greeting. He didn't respond.

A smaller green cross was lit at the back of the store, and I wandered back to where a young woman with long braided hair was sorting listlessly through a wall of tiny drawers.

"Hi. Is this the pharmacy?"

She paused between drawers, inspecting me. "Yeah."

"I have some chemicals to pick up. Some are prescribed by the medical station, and some were ordered by the Institute for Terrestrial Biology."

"Scan your wearable." She waved towards a small device with a red light at the edge of the counter separating us.

"Okay."

The recognition chime of my bracelet assistant brought her to the terminal interface, where a frown grew on her face. "Your system history starts three days ago, but it says your standard age is thirty-six. You scamming drugs?"

I blinked. "No, I'm in a receptacle body. I only finished beaming to Nordenmark from Earth three days ago."

"Oh. You're the Earth scientist." Her full attention was on me now, eyes roving over my face, body, searching my neck for the little blue circle of light that signified an artificial brain was connected. Weighing me inside this new context.

I nodded, examining the drawers behind her, drumming my fingers against the side of the counter, trying not to shrink from her scrutiny.

"What's it like there? Does everyone have their hair like that?"

"Uh…not everyone." I stammered, cheeks flushing. What was Earth like? Flashes of the frozen desert, the gravel peaks of the mountains, the clear scalding burn of the summer sun. My temple began to throb. *Did* everyone have their hair like this? I couldn't think straight. The bones of my fingers ached from clinging to the side of the counter. She waited. "There's too many different places to sum it all up. I'm from the north of the Canadian desert. It's dry there."

She nodded, tapping through the terminal screen. At least with her focus there I felt less conspicuous. "I really can't imagine leaving a stable place like Earth for Nordenmark."

I forced a smile. With the pain drilling into my head, I had no idea what I had left behind. "I've only been inside the medical station and here so far, but the greenery is a nice change."

"Yeah, well, they're saying everything here is going to die out, so enjoy it while it lasts." She looked up from the terminal, expression blank. "It's going to take some time to synthesize these, I don't recognize the chemistry."

"The list from the station or from ITB?" It was getting hard to breathe again, my heart pounding. This small body was proving difficult.

Her frown deepened. "Both. I've never heard of postbeam stabilization chemistry or these chaperonin granules. What are they for?"

"Environmental treatment." Too little, too late. "Do you think you can prioritize the stabilization compounds?" The room began to pulse. I needed to get out, get somewhere I could breathe.

She looked doubtful. "I might be able to have them ready late tomorrow. It depends on how much trouble they are to synthesize. The other chemicals, probably another two days."

"Okay, sure. I'll come back for them then."

Her eyes were on my neck again as I backed away from the counter. "Watch your wearable, you'll get a ping when they're done."

Hiding in the privacy of the tall aisles, I picked out cricket flour bread, small brown lentils, and sprouts, the assistant scolding my heart for beating too fast. The desert, the feel of sand between my teeth, slithered out of my mind's grasp. Images of Earth, of Canada, should have been crystal clear. I reached the far end of the store, where long rows of dark cooling units sat empty. The shelves were still covered in labels, signs for sheep's milk and goat cheese, fermented yogurts and meats. A stark announcement of the decimation of the livestock in Godhavn.

I leaned against the empty cases and tried to breathe, tried to think.

The preparation lab I had been in on Earth had pale blue flooring. Long rows of blinking transfer devices next to a white hospital bed. Amber-coloured tubes. I was there alone. Was there supposed to be a technician, or a nurse maybe? There was an absence. I couldn't remember if there was someone there or no one at all.

The shoots in my hand snapped in half, and I started. Their green centres oozed over my palm where I had crushed them.

––––––––

Out in the grey streets again, the assistant led me through Godhavn to the last door in a deserted row house, then up some stairs into a small apartment. A single naked light flickered on as my heartbeat registered, illuminating a low bed against an empty wall and a small kitchenette. I leaned against the door, letting the sack of food drop, slowing my breath to calm my new heart. The humid air pushed at dark curtains across the open window, revealing an eye, watching me.

We stared at each other.

"Well hello. How did you get in here?"

The lizard blinked at me in response, one leg frozen above the floor, mid-step. She was easily as long as my arm, a velvety black decorated with white dots along her belly, though dead skin rippled out in gauzy layers, incompletely shed. Dysecdysis. The word was immediate, clear. She looked malnourished.

"Don't worry, you can stay if you like," I told the lizard. "You might need someone to help you with that skin, though. Maybe there's something for you to have a soak in here…" The kitchen drawers held a total of three splintered chopsticks, a knife, two ceramic plates, a fan, and a sealed cardboard box of linens.

"Not much to start a life on," I told her, opening the empty cooling unit. Setting the groceries inside only made it look emptier. I pulled one of the oozing green shoots from its bundle and tossed it towards my watcher. She took a tentative step out from the curtain, keeping an eye on the intruder in her home. "Go ahead. You look like you need it."

The upper cupboards held a solitary glass. I filled it with water from the dehumidifier unit, continuing my search in the bathroom, a closet with brown tile and pale green fixtures. The sink was too shallow to fit the lizard. Judging by the desiccated spiders on the countertop, no human had been in this apartment for a long time.

"Not much in here either."

The tiny cabinet behind the mirror was full, crammed with expired vitamin supplements and antifungal cream, a stale smart bandage and a tarnished piece of coppery jewellery. A pendant shaped like a teardrop resting on top of a T.

"Wonder what happened to the last person," I mused, poking through the ephemera. When I turned around, the lizard was halfway underneath the bed. "Maybe you knew them. You're pretty big, you must have seen what's been going on around here. Everything falling apart. Any tips for how to fix this, Hecate?"

The name came out of my mouth like a good friend's. I rolled it over my tongue again and again. Hecate. Its familiarity was overwhelming. I couldn't remember ever meeting someone named that. My head felt thick, aching as I dredged the depths of my brain for where I knew the name from. The more I searched, the more slippery everything became, faces of technical staff and classmates bleeding together and fissioning.

I leaned against the sink, focused on the lizard's tail retreating, trying to recall. The apartment wavered, threatening to spin.

Hecate's eye glinted from the shadow.

A wave of adrenaline sent my heart thundering, darkness pulsing at the sides of my vision. Gripping the sink, I exhaled, slowly, forcing it back to calm.

"Gods, it feels like this body is dying." I sank down to the floor, resting my head against the tile wall. Damask lizards were omnivorous; hopefully she hadn't left the shoots behind to wait for something tastier.

We sat together until the room felt solid again, the pain in my temple subsided. I pushed my hair off my face, adjusted the jumpsuit Eva had given me.

"Thanks for sticking around. I guess I lied to you about staying, you'll have to come up to the Institute with me. There isn't anything we can soak you in here."

I dumped the contents of the linens box onto the kitchen counter, and set it on the floor on its side. The image of holding a small box with a plastic bag in it flashed, incongruous, driving the pain in my temple to a hot whine. I pushed it away, focusing on Hecate's face poking out from the near side of the bed. This body tired easily; if I wanted to carry this lizard anywhere, I would have to go soon.

"What do you think? It's the only thing here."

The lizard took a tentative step forward.

Kneeling next to the bed, I ushered Hecate into the box, soft chirping noises coming from under the flaps as I closed them.

"I know. But I promise you'll be more comfortable. And it's better than wasting away in this place."

I tucked the box under my arm and walked out of the apartment—my apartment—and into the dim streets. It was early evening, the weak light of the Nordenmark star casting long shadows between the plants that climbed up the row houses, the ground littered with pieces of the wooden roofs pulled down by their vines. Insects crawled the warm roads; moths and crane flies wove clumsy patterns in the thick air.

The assistant pinged directions as Hecate and I walked through the gathering night, red lamps turning on in the streets. The cloudy sky turned black, the four tiny satellites of Nordenmark too small to give any moonlight. Dark shapes of the people of Godhavn moved around us, tired faces shifting along the street or watching us from where they sat in yards outside the housing units. We left them behind at a cemetery, where rows of small stone or wood crosses were choked by forest overgrowth. I carried Hecate through the crumbling facades of abandoned dead until my feet found the path that led up to the Institute for Terrestrial Biology.

3

The forest was dark, the groans of wood-boring in-sects loud against the quiet night. Tiny flies stuck to my exposed skin, bumped into my face as I followed the assistant's directions, blind. My unsteady feet found their way through the dark until the faint sound of de-humidifier vents emerged. As the sound grew closer, I saw a weak glow cast against the forest, a faint red that I thought I imagined until it resolved into windows where the indoor light was shielded from spilling out into the forest. The insects here were sensitive to changes in their photoperiod, I had read that somewhere in the preparation dossiers. The shielding made the building almost invisible. We found our way to a heavy door and a chime from the assistant opened it, revealing a long, grey-tiled entrance. I could feel Hecate shifting inside the box, restless.

"We're almost there."

The assistant led us down a set of stairs, my footsteps echoing, the air cooling as we descended into a hall lined with solid doors. The panel of one lit up green as we approached, the magnetic lock releasing with a click.

Inside was a laboratory space not unlike what I was used to back on Earth. Benches ran the length of the room, and the walls were papered in diagrams of vertebrate anatomy. Prepared skeletons of bats and felids and sheep stood underneath them.

I set Hecate down and opened the top of the box. She didn't look too stressed by the journey, at least. For a wild creature, that was saying something.

"Hello?" a voice said. From behind the benches, a man rose. He was slight, with black hair that curled around his ears, a startled look on his face.

"Oh, I didn't realize someone was in here. I'm Inga Nyström. The assistant let me in."

"Ah." His eyes narrowed for a second. "I didn't recognize you."

I nodded. "Yeah, me neither. They didn't have time to grow the receptacle body all the way. I don't look like I did on Earth." Amidst piles of grimy specimen jars and dusty storage cartridges I spotted a tub that was the perfect size for Hecate.

"Ah," he said again. "I'm Amit Sandhu."

"The veterinarian."

He nodded, rubbing his forehead with the back of his hand. "Welcome to hell. What's in the box?"

"Damask lizard, I think. She was inside my apartment when I got here, I brought her in to get rid of some of the shed that's clinging to her. She's in rough shape."

Amit walked around the bench to peer into the box, the lizard creeping over the bottom, her velvety black skin inky between the dead patches. "They pretty much all are these days."

"So I heard. Wish I would have been here sooner." I pulled the tub down and began to fill it at the sink.

He shook his head. "Things fell apart so quickly, I don't know what you could have done."

"I'm so sorry." I ran my hand under the water, checking that it was warm. "I thought I'd be consulting on recovery efforts and arthropod control, but the assignment I have now is to calculate the total species remaining in the Godhavn biome and document as many of their genomes as possible. It's...awful." The list of species to collect genetic data from had been a shock — a handful of reptiles, six species of fish, no birds, a short list of mammals. The preliminary estimates suggested no more than a third of the seeded Nordenmark vertebrate species might still be resisting extinction.

Amit nodded as I set the tub on the bench. "She's big. Doesn't seem too distressed from the journey."

"Hecate." The taste of her name on my tongue held the same strange familiarity it had in the apartment. The room pulsed.

Amit looked up, coolly studying my face. "Chthonian goddess of liminal spaces. Fitting."

The familiarity swelled, bringing a flash of pain back to my temple. I swallowed, steadying myself against the cool steel of the bench. "Yeah, I guess."

"You alright?"

"Yeah." The pain was supposed to be going away. "Just taking a bit to adjust to the new brain. Can you help me lift her?"

Together we scooped Hecate up and set her into the tub, her yellow tongue flicking out over the water. Amit inspected the skin around her face, her eyes rolling between the two of us.

"She probably has mites and other parasites to be looking this malnourished. The forest is overwhelmed with insects with the bat and lizard populations as they are."

I sighed. "I thought we were in this together, Hecate." Rubbing at the springy surface of my printed skull did nothing for the pain.

"She might yet survive. Hecate has the rare distinction of living with one of Earth's foremost parasitologists." I looked up at Amit's solemn face, my mouth dry. He gave a wry smile. "Might survive for a while, anyways. We're not very far into solving the mysteries of damask lizard mortality."

"From this headache, I'm not sure if we're as far as we think in extending human lifespans. Is there any place to make some tea around here?"

Amit nodded, stroking Hecate's head with a finger. Her eyes were half-closed; she was enjoying the warm bath. "Hecate seems content here. I'll show you around."

———

We walked through the maze of hallways in the basement, under buzzing lights and humming vats of liquid nitrogen, past locked doors with dark windows. It seemed only Amit and I were around, and I said as much.

"Yeah, it's pretty dead here now. We don't have many embryos left in cryostorage from what was brought on the generation ship from Earth—some birds, a few mammals." He gestured along the hall. "At the beginning, there was a big effort to replace the sheep and goats and deer that died. But now there's no point in bringing anything up unless the collapse can be stabilized."

I nodded, and we walked in silence past abandoned laboratories and empty vivariums. Amit didn't look that old, maybe his early thirties. Choosing veterinary medicine on a planet on the brink of ecological collapse was brave. He bent to push in the loose metal edging on a door that wouldn't close, revealing a tattoo on the back of his neck. A teardrop resting on top of a T, the same shape as the pendant in my apartment.

We ended up in a small kitchen just off the laboratory. The ceiling was filled with green glass blocks that filtered light from the floor above, reflecting as an eerie glow on the metal kitchen implements. I sank into a chair while Amit filled a glass from the sweating water tank, handed me a small box with satchels of herbs in mesh spheres. He sat on the counter, legs swinging as I steeped a strong-smelling bundle of dark green leaves.

"The disinfectant smells the same here as on Earth," I said.

"I expect there are a lot of things that are still similar between Nordenmark and Earth even after 200-odd years of people living here. Everything except the rocks and water was imported: animals, disinfectant recipes. Prions." He winced, looked up to the green glass of the ceiling. "Guess they forgot about those when they designed the Godhavn biome. But you know about all that."

I tried to give a friendly nod as the room throbbed again.

"You sure you're alright?"

"Yeah." I sat up straight, puffed out my shrunken lungs to their capacity. "I think so. The transfer was just a bit rough."

"Your hands are shaking." Amit pointed, and I wrapped them tight around the warm glass. He hopped down from the counter and slid into the chair opposite mine, eyes focused on my pupils, fingers on my pulse. "When's the last time you ate? Did they mention any blood pressure problems because of the incomplete growth of the receptacle body?"

No use evading someone trained to treat beings that couldn't speak.

"It's not that, there's something off about the heart, an arrhythmia maybe. Eva, the lead transfer doctor, said it should stabilize over the next few days."

"Ah," Amit said, leaning back. I sipped at the tea. The strong taste eased the ache. A little. "If you want, I can hook you up to one of the large animal heart monitors. Otherwise, there's painkillers, stimulants, electrolytes, a resting room... What aggravates it?"

"I'm not sure..." I tried to think back. It had started after trying to remember who was in the transfer room on Earth. Was there a problem with my heart right before transfer? It skipped a beat. The spinning was coming back. I tried to shake it off, change the subject. I pointed to the back of my neck. "Your tattoo. I found an old pendant with the same symbol in the vanity at my apartment. What is it?"

Amit gave that wry smile again. "It's an ankh. The key of life."

I shook my head. Another deep slow breath to quiet the erratic fluttering in my chest. "What's that?"

"A symbol from ancient Earth. People here wear it sometimes as a talisman for life to persist on Nordenmark." He cocked his head at me. "You named your lizard Hecate but you haven't seen an ankh?"

"I don't really know where the name came from either." I rubbed my sternum, slowing my exhale. "Gods, this heart is trying to escape or something."

"Whoa there." Amit reached across to steady me as I tried to stand up, to escape the crushing feeling in my chest. "Maybe just sit for a second, I'll ping the medical station. You said the transfer doc's name was Eva?"

"It's fine, I just need to get some air—" I started, pushing the chair back. Amit tapped at the wearable on his wrist and caught my elbow as I wavered. A voice asked what assistance was needed. I couldn't hear Amit's response.

The chair toppled, and the luminous green of the ceiling pulsed crazily with my heartbeat.

I returned to the howling of the frozen, empty darkness.

4

I gasped, launching upwards out of the terror of the abyss into the blinding light of the medical station. There was a stinging inside my chest, an electric foam bubbling against my ribs. Eva's worried face watched me as I panted for air.

"Deep breaths, Inga, you're alright."

"This can't be alright." I grunted. The air wasn't coming in fast enough. My fingers found a wound opposite the blue circle of light in my chest, numbed beyond feeling. Panic squeezed at my heart. "What's this, what's happening?"

She shook her head. "You have to believe that I trained so hard for this, but no one's ever been transferred to Nordenmark before. I've been scouring every database I can and…I don't know. Your heart just stops beating. It just stops. We've had to put in a depolarizer implant for now to restart it, to keep you with us."

Eva hooked a rolling stool with her foot and sat down, her blue eyes looking into mine. They were sad. The way she stroked the tattoo of a baby's footprints on her arm, an ankh resting between the two tiny arches, told me this wasn't going to be good news.

"What is it."

"I don't know anything for sure." Eva tapped the terminal monitoring my vitals. It flipped to a display of the artificial brain that sat inside my skull, numbers and networks sparkling. "Every part of your brain's molecular structure was transferred here—your personality, memory, enzyme states, control of your kidney function—and we grew the receptacle body from your genome and microbiome, so everything must be the same. Or...should be." She faltered. "You didn't have a heart arrhythmia on Earth, but my scans here show that you do. And I can't find any reason for it. But if the only thing that's different is your brain...I wondered...if that might be where the problem is."

I blinked. "They've transferred all sorts of things into replicated brains, though. Frogs. Mice. Pigs, sheep..." It felt like there were more, but my mind drew a blank. I shook it off. "It's the most studied part of beam-transfer."

"I know...it's just..." Eva tapped the side of her head. "It's just that when I scanned you, I think I found a...a dead space. Inside your brain. A cluster of neurocels with no activity."

"Did they not have time to activate the neurites at your synthesis labs?" The words dripped with incredulity. Defective. *Fragile.* I spat them at her.

"I don't think it's the synthesis that's caus—"

"I can barely breathe, I'm dizzy, this heart keeps stopping. This is my *brain*, Eva. Everything I brought from Earth is in there."

"I know. I'm so sorry, Inga." The sincerity of the tears in her eyes filled me with disgust, and more anger that I knew she wasn't responsible for. I turned away.

"Do you know the function of the dead space?" My reflection in the glossy sterile wall opposite stared back at me, the black hair I knew so well jutting over a foreign, collapsed body.

Eva's reflection chewed her lip. "No, I don't. There are still impulses that travel towards those cels, but they just disappear. From the physiological symptoms you're having, if I had to guess, maybe it's something with an instinctual component to it. But there's no way to know what. There's been so few people transferred, and nothing like this has ever happened before. There's no protocol."

"So I'm stuck with a hole in my head." The words were cold. My hands felt numb. I had known the risk. It had seemed worth it when there was something left I could do for Nordenmark. Now that there wasn't, I wanted everything that was missing back.

"I'm sending an update to Earth about this, I can ask them if they have information they can send you, some way to figure out or relearn what's missing. But the delay one way is nine days, so this won't be fast, or easy... and it's hard to predict what will happen with your heart..." Eva's face was mottled as she stared down at her hands, anxious. It was hard to predict how much time I had to try and fix this.

"What else is there to do. If they don't know what's gone, or how to fix it...that's that."

"I could maybe try giving you an antidepressant, see if that will ease some of the symptoms." Her deep-set eyes finally met mine. "A high dose might have some effect on your neurotransmitter concentrations."

"No." I picked at the seam of the blanket. "Like you said, nothing like this has ever happened before. It might help, it might do nothing, it might make things worse."

We sat in silence.

It was daylight outside the window, the star a small, pale disc behind the ever-present wash of grey clouds respiring through the city. The building across from the medical station faded into the sky, the dark ductwork on the roof appearing and disappearing in the ebb and flow of the fog.

"When can I be cleared to go?" I asked the window.

———

When I left the medical station the next day, my bracelet chimed twice. The first was the assistant telling me the food in my cooling unit had spoiled. The second was a ping from Amit: a capture of Hecate basking under a heat lamp in the lab.

The day was sticky and damp, but early, and there were eighteen more days until a response from Earth might arrive. Might as well head back to the Institute, start on the assignment I had lost so much for.

———

I left the anaesthetic hum of the city streets and the rows of crowded houses, their windows hanging open, weaving past repair shops and recycling depots and charging stations until I found the cemetery at the edge of the path up to the Institute. I was alone, and in the daylight, the broken rows of gravestones were peaceful. I stopped to pull branches and vines off them and read the epitaph for Anders, beloved father. Elisabet, who introduced eighty-five species of plants. Baby Bengtsson, taken too soon. Weeds had already sprung up on a recent grave dug at one end, and as I approached it the sharp image flashed again: my hands opening a small box, plastic inside holding dark earth. I sagged against a tree, holding my chest until my heart rate subsided, the pain in my temple eased, and I had the strength to leave and walk into the muggy gloom of the forest.

It was quiet enough to hear the fog drip falling from the canopy, thudding onto the dirt. Fish flies stuck to my neck, their translucent bodies tracing weak loops around the damp bushes, my bare arms. Inspecting the strange mammal in their empty forest.

"Most of you should be in the stomach of a bird," I murmured.

At the Institute, I made my way to the laboratory and found Amit balanced in a chair on its two back legs. Dark circles had been etched into the space under his eyes since I last saw him.

"Ah. You're alive," he said, bringing the front two legs of the chair to the floor.

"Partially, at least." I brushed the clinging fish flies off my jumpsuit, inspected my arms. There was still a pulse in them.

"I cleared a desk off for you while I was on call last night." He gestured at a heavy table with a terminal, a line of glass jars, and a prepared bat skeleton with wing bones extending wide on either side of the terminal's screen. Its jaw was open in a snarl. I picked up a worn paper book sitting underneath it.

"*Gods of Pre-Anthropocene Earth*?" I asked.

He rubbed at his eyes. "It's pretty old, but there's a few pages on Hecate in there."

"Thanks, Amit. You alright?"

His cheek twitched. "Yeah. Tired. A guy brought in a deer from Vargholmen yesterday. It didn't make it."

"That's rough. I'm sorry." I poked through the things lining the back of the table. One of the glass jars on the desk held a translucent, segmented tapeworm, the hooked mouthparts of the intestinal parasite just large enough to be visible. There was a piece of peeling tape on the side, YUM written in big block letters.

"Ah, it's always the same end for cervids. Has been for some time. It's a good sign there are still deer out there, to be honest."

"That's a pragmatic way of looking at it." The tub we had soaked Hecate in was empty, drying upside down on the side of the laboratory sink. A heat lamp glowed red over a large tank I hadn't seen before. "How's Hecate?"

"She's better. The bath helped with the dysecdysis. She's been a little more active, though she hasn't eaten much yet."

"Guess I should take a sample from her. Preserve the genome of the Nordenmark damask lizard." I ran my fingers along the long spindles of the bat's flight bones. "Who's this? She's enormous."

"Modgunn. She's from before my time, before the bigger bats died off." He rested his head on a hand. "She's in the book too, an ancient goddess who holds dominion over the river between the living and the dead. Thought you'd like her as a companion."

"Modgunn," I murmured. There was a twinge in my temple, a ricochet heartbeat inside my chest. I had no idea if I did or didn't know her. Now that I knew it existed, the empty space inside my brain threatened to swallow up memories and truths, pulling at the threads of myself. I sank into the desk chair, staring into the hissing bat skull, tiny fragile bone of the eye sockets level with my own. "Gods, I'm not sure."

"Ah, I thought with a lizard named Hecate—"

I waved him off. "No, don't worry, it's nice." I sighed, running my fingers through my hair. Parts of it were still sticky from Eva's scan leads. "I think. I'm actually not sure. Eva—the doctor at the medical station—said there's a dead space in my brain."

Amit leaned back and stared at me, chair squeaking. "Ah. What was in there?"

"We don't know. Something important I guess, without it this heart keeps stopping, and I collapse, like in the kitchen before."

He frowned. "Is there something they can do to fix it?"

"Don't know that either. Have to wait for Earth to respond."

"That's rough. I'm sorry, Inga."

"Well. More room to store the whereabouts of all the wildlife here."

He was silent at that.

"Anyway. I should start to get things set up to run genome sequencing."

"The beginning of the end," murmured Amit. "If you're after recent samples, I still have to prepare the deer before it goes into the chemical digester."

"Prepare?" I frowned. "What are you using in the digestion mix that a carcass needs preparation?"

"Oh, no, not that type of preparation. More like a sort of funeral, I guess. Not the traditional three-week wake, just the wayfinding. And the candy."

I stared at him. "The candy."

"The little sugar corpses in black fringed paper?"

I shook my head. I was sure there was nothing in the Nordenmark cultural dossier about this. But then again, maybe it had been in the hole in my head.

"Well. If you want, you can see what might be the last Godhavn deer." Amit gave that wry smile. "And experience Nordenmark funeral customs firsthand. But only if you want to."

"Yeah, of course I'll come with you."

Amit nodded. His voice held levity, but the circles under his eyes carried years of death. Not from of the skeletons lined up around the lab, but of an entire species, one individual after another. For the first time, as we walked out of the lab, my feet felt the weight carried by the Godhavn people.

––––––––

Another concrete maze led us closer to the smell of disinfectant, harsher here than around the laboratory. At a set of locked doors Amit stopped and took two small packages out of his pocket.

"One for you and one for me. We have to wear gear in the next area because of the prion."

He placed a small form wrapped in thin black paper into my hand. Each end was shredded into a short fringe, with the flat side bearing a small picture of a grave, a heart and anchor lying on each side of the central silver cross. I unwrapped it and found a pale hard sugar corpse inside, the ridges of its skull crumbling against the tissue. There was a piece of white paper wound around the tiny body. I pulled it out and read the rhyme written in miniature script.

"The dark, quiet abyss;
All our days will end like this."

"It's my favourite of the funeral rhymes." Amit popped his sugar corpse into his mouth. "You'll need two pairs of gloves, gown, respirator, and goggles to go past the airlock. Nobody's gotten sick with any sort of variant encephalopathy so far, so the prion doesn't seem transmissible to humans, but just be careful."

"Okay."

We suited up and passed into the white hall beyond, walking until we reached a door with a window covered in red film, hazard codes and symbols in black on red squares along the top of the doorframe. Someone had taped up a paper square with an ankh beside them. A talisman for life in a morgue.

As soon as Amit opened the door, the air around us changed. Even through the respirator I could smell the acrid gases of the digester, the chemical stew that reduced matter to its elemental components.

The deer lay on a padded bed in the center of the room, legs curled up underneath it. It would have looked like it was sedated, its velvet nose oblivious to the stench in the bare concrete room, but for the angle of its head, the skull pulled over by the weight of the antlers, tongue lolling out. The knobs of its spine stuck through its skin in a ridge that led to a white-tufted tail. Wasting disease was the right word for it.

"Poor little guy." My words were muffled through the respirator.

"Yeah." Amit ran his gloved hand over the tawny fur on its shoulder. I stroked one of its ears. "Biopsy kit is in that drawer. What do you want to sample?"

"Some muscle...and prescapular lymph nodes for prion load, I guess."

Amit wrapped his arms around the deer and gently pulled its leg up out of the way. I cut through the skin, over the bone, and as I felt for the node through my incision, I saw Amit's thumb stroking the deer's lifeless leg where he held it. Comforting a scared animal.

The grips brought the smooth grey of the lymph node through the congealing blood, and I dropped it into a fluid-filled specimen jar. For Amit, I closed the incision with neat stitches, tied off.

"Done."

Amit replaced the deer's leg, and as I changed my bloody gloves, he lit a small gas burner and placed it on the table alongside a small tin and brush. He peeked at me over the respirator, putting a hand on the deer's shoulder.

"So…first there's the address to the dead, then marking of the wayfinder." He cleared his throat. "I wish we could bury you outside in a forest filled with your kin, that your body would return to the ground instead of your atoms broken down in here. I hope that some day your kind will run again through the forest."

Amit took the tin and brush and painted four bright white lines intersecting on the ribs over the heart of the deer, decorating each spoke of the rune with shorter lines and arrows. It was reverent. I grasped at bits of funerals I had attended on Earth, retrieving only blurred pieces, and nothing like this. A red scarf worn to celebrate the life of a teacher, a memorial tree with oval leaves, a white coffin lowered into the desert. The box of dark earth seared into my mind, disintegrating in my hands, floating away like ash. With it came the staggering pain in my temple. I pushed it away, focused on the deer.

"He's ready now." Amit put the lid back onto the tin.

"*The dark, quiet abyss; All our days will end like this,*" I murmured.

Amit nodded and pulled hard at the handle of a massive hatch set in the side of the wall, wrenching it open. The smell that came from the pit inside made my nose burn, my eyes water, but I helped Amit push the bed to its mouth, load the deer into its throat. We closed the door together on the carcass, tears streaming from my eyes. The sound of mechanical grinding came from beyond the walls and a glass panel above the door illuminated orange, the letters of the word DIGESTION swimming in my tears.

The room warmed as chemical reactions began dismantling the deer, heat wavering off the metal face of the door. We stood at the door until the grinding slowed to a stop. I waited until Amit gave a little nod and turned off the gas burner.

The silence in the corridor on the way back to the airlock amplified the pounding in my head until I couldn't bear it.

"I read that my body on Earth went into a digester. After I was encoded for transfer."

I heard Amit's head snap towards me, but he said nothing.

"Anyway, there's only here for me now. I hope, for all our sakes, that wasn't the last deer in Godhavn."

5

The air was sticky and close inside the apartment, a listless wind sucking the curtains against the open window, rustling Amit's book of old-world gods on the countertop. I was supposed to be out in Vargholmen checking beaver dams already, but the windows of species counts floated on my mobile terminal, abandoned. My assistant chimed warnings for dehydration, for reduced function due to sleeplessness, for something called fog lightning, and still I lay there.

The response from Earth was late.

Twenty days since Eva sent off the message about the hole in my brain. Whatever they sent back here, they had taken two days so far to prepare it. The thought of it itched. I pushed my limp hair out of my eyes and rolled over the sweat-damp bed.

"What is taking them so long."

Hecate looked at me from her perch on a massive piece of deadwood I had brought in for her. Her skin was a lustrous, velvety black, and she had gained some weight. Amit warned me it wouldn't last. The mites and worms and other parasites had damaged her heart, she was dying. I couldn't do anything to help her. The tick box next to damask lizard was checked, genome captured. That was all.

"Earth, I mean. Is there a new development, are they sending a new generation ship? Did they just forget?" I asked her, standing up at last. I had imagined twenty days of journals, lab notebooks, reels and images, obscure geometric formulas or muscle memory that would fill in the empty spot in my head. The feel of the sun was getting hard to conjure under Godhavn's pale, cloudy sky, I needed something to hold on to, to fill the absence that lurked on the edge of my vision. As if summoned, the small cardboard box flashed behind my eyes, the plastic bag inside filled with black dust. Disjointed voices, the unbearable pain. I took a deep breath and focussed on Hecate's flickering yellow tongue, the feel of the jumpsuit in my clenched hands, the smell of spruce and sweat. Deep breaths, slowing my heartbeat. Gritting my teeth as I put my boots on. Calm down. Avoid the sting of the depolarizer.

I said goodbye to Hecate, promised to be back soon, told her she'd been a good friend. Our ritual, in preparation for the last time.

———————

The teeth marks on the stumps were old. Wherever I found a gnawed tree, the splintered wood had long since browned, or was dark green with fungus. There was nothing inside the mounds of sticks that clotted the boggy stream, the calculated number of Nordenmark beavers remained zero. I wandered downstream, past thick trees that hid everything except cooling towers from what the assistant said was Godhavn Sedimentary Basin Gas Refinery 4. At one point the stream was cut by a looming stone barrier, water seeping through pipes too small to enter. I walked around it, turned one way or another by metal fences threaded with vines and yards with piles of gravel and scrap. Leading a swarm of flies and moths through the muggy forest.

Sweating and bug-eaten, I found the stream again where it opened onto a lake, the shoreline spreading into a park area with wooden tables and benches. The gnawing ache had grown inside my chest, so I sat down to catch my breath, staring into the white-grey reflection of cloud in the lake surface. I was being eaten away, from inside and out.

A clattering noise broke my thoughts, followed by a sharp prod in my arm.

I turned to find a black bird inspecting me.

A bird. I was stunned. He was magnificent, black feathers shimmering a deep iridescent blue. He gave a throaty croak and bounced away on taloned feet, flapping up to a branch above. The call was returned from a table on the other side of the clearing, half-hidden in the fog, where other birds fluttered about a figure that raised a hand.

"Sorry 'bout that. Garmr's a bit confused there, thinks you're a tree."

I wiped my forehead on the back of my hand. "That's alright."

The words had barely left my mouth when Garmr plummeted from the branch, bouncing with a heavy thud. The figure ran forward, swearing, picking the bird up and prying at its head.

"What are you doing, you'll kill it!" I cried, aghast.

They laughed, a deep chuckle, and brought the bird towards me. The beautiful face of a teenager resolved out of the fog, scalp perfectly smooth. Their shoulders were broad, muscular, a star-spattered shirt hanging from them, their fingernails painted a deep red. They smiled and held Garmr towards me, pushing his feathers aside with two thumbs. Carbon fiber casing pocked with screwheads peeked through.

"No harm done, see? Garmr's an automaton." The other birds jeered, bickering amongst themselves, surrounding us in the thrum of beating wings. "They all are. I'd have freaked too though; I haven't seen a real crow alive here for a long time. Actually, I was back and forth between a crow and a bat when I was making these guys, but I've read that crows would make friends with humans more often than bats would, so I figured it would be more natural. Are you lost?"

The question was abrupt. I brushed at the thorny sticks clinging to my jumpsuit.

"Oh. No, I'm out here trying to find a beaver. Garmr's beautiful though... Looks just like a real crow."

A wash of suspicion played over their face. "The last crow died sixty years ago. Where did you see a crow?"

"I'm Inga Nyström. There were a lot of crows on Earth." I held out my hand, which was carefully shaken.

"I'm Freja, or Frej, Ek." Freja nodded at the crows surrounding us, and dug their thumbs into Garmr's neck. "The rest of them don't have names yet. Garmr was the first."

There was a click from under Frej's hands and the automaton crow came to life, kicking its feet. He flew up into the tree and scolded us, the harsh sound echoing over the lake. It recalled fragments of Earth memories, black birds dotting a bright blue winter sky. A wave of nausea crested and I gritted my teeth, trying to focus on anything else.

"Where have you seen a real crow if the last one died sixty years ago?" I asked.

Freja squinted at me. "You don't know the Skellefteå program?"

I shook my head. "No, sorry."

"I figured they would have told you, but whatever, not many people remember it now. It's been something like a hundred and twelve years, I think. Nordenmark was supposed to receive the first beamed person from Earth, so the Institute for Terrestrial Biology had a transferred consciousness program. They worked on a lot of the beam coding, tested things over short distances and all that, but they ran out of cobalt because of an estimation error in the mineral scans when they started terraforming. But anyways, since they couldn't develop the program further here, it got scrapped and sent to Risha. So Wei Song was the first person beamed, from Earth to Risha."

I was sure I had studied the history of the technology that had brought me here, but there was only a whisper of it in my memory. A flash of what I thought could be Wei Song's face, but that was all. "Sorry, what does that have to do with you seeing crows?"

Frej pulled the neck of their shirt to the side, exposing a luminous blue circle just above the skin of their collarbone. The black of carbon fiber bone stretched out their pale skin underneath it.

I stared.

"I'm the last participant of the Skellefteå transfer program. I was here before the crows went extinct, that's where I saw them."

The air came out of my shallow lungs in a rush. I wasn't the only one. My head oozed with questions as I stared at the subcutaneous light.

"You were transferred. From where?"

Freja held a hand out to one of the crow automatons. It hopped up and began to preen its feathers. "From Godhavn. I was sixteen, I had an aggressive leukemia, and my parents worked at ITB. Half privilege, half bad luck." They stroked the crow's head for a moment. "Sorry if that's all jumbled up, I didn't think I'd meet you so soon. Kind of figured there was time, that us two would be a constant on Nordenmark. I've outlived the rest of the participants and might have another few centuries yet. It's nice to meet you."

"Nice to meet you too," I managed. Another few centuries. A flare of rage caught me off guard. I was supposed to have that time, but instead I was anxious about lasting weeks. The apparent teenager lifted their arm, and the crow took flight, shrieking as it fluttered to the ground and began fighting another bird for the carapace of a wood borer. "How was your transfer?"

Frej shrugged. "Just like they say, it was like being reborn. Made a big improvement not to be so tired and sick all the time. How was yours?"

I bit my tongue, swallowing my venom until I was sure I wasn't going to explode at Freja. "Uh…there were some complications."

"Oh, I'm sorry to hear that." It seemed genuine, but face-to-face with a successfully transferred person, the heat of my envy burned.

As I opened my mouth to brush it off, the wearable chimed, my heart spiking with its staccato tones.

Eva.

"Inga?" She was breathless. "The response from Earth is coming through. It'll be another hour or two until it's fully here and decoded. Can you come to the medical station?"

"I'm in Vargholmen, but I'll be there right away." I looked at Frej. "It's a response from Earth about those transfer complications. I need to head back into the city, but can I ping you sometime?"

"Don't have a wearable," Freja said. "But I come out here with the murder every day. Don't be a stranger."

I gave them what I hoped was a smile. "What's the closest way to the tram?"

Frej pointed along the shoreline. "Ten minutes along the shore, until you see the sign."

"Thanks. See you around." I heaved off the bench and started along the shoreline. Behind me, I could hear Freja chirruping softly to the crows until the fog swallowed the sound.

The tram rattled through the forest, branches scratching along the windows of the deserted car. The trees were broken by overgrown fields with leaning fences, scars of black earth where the herds that used to graze there had been burned and buried. As dusk fell, the farmhouse windows remained dark. The forests here were mature and lush, but no one lived out on the land anymore.

By the time I got back into Godhavn the dark air was still, the wind too weak to dry the glistening trees or scatter the swarms of flies. The yards I passed choked, dark vines and weeds creeping in to smother open doors and windows. Sounds of infotainment and digital worlds escaped into the street, bright screens broken with the dark silhouettes of people. My boots thumped past them, alone.

I found Eva at the medical station, pacing in front of her terminal. Waiting.

"It's not finished decoding yet," she warned me. "Eight percent still to go. I know it's not going to help watching it, but I'm paranoid it's not going to come through intact."

She chattered about the Earth–Nordenmark beamline while I sank into a chair. Eight percent until some answers, something to fill in the space in my head. I watched the progress, my skin prickling as it dried in the dehumidified air.

"There we go. Six percent. Gods, it's so close now. They better have something helpful in there."

I nodded.

While Eva fussed with the terminal, closing documents and preparing notes, I watched in heavy silence. My hands were slick with sweat. Time stretched. Each percentage point was agonizing.

At last, a package resolved on Eva's terminal screen.

"It's here." She laughed, sighing in relief as she opened the folder to reveal four documents. "Yes, the file sizes are what they should be, it made it, it's all here. Where do you want to start?"

My dream of a rich collection of my life on Earth began to evaporate. One single document was titled with my name, the smallest of the four by far. I took a deep breath. "That one, the one with my name on it."

Eva nodded. "I'd do the same. I'll give you a minute, I should call my kid and check in that he's alright anyways. I'll just be outside if you need me."

I took another deep breath, trying to buoy my sinking heart, and with shaking hands opened the document. It wasn't a big file. It wasn't the substance to fill in the empty part of my brain. The text took up less than half the terminal screen.

Re: Transfer anomaly

We have received the report detailing the circumstances of your transfer. After careful diagnostics we have uncovered a deviation due to a faulty transfer core that caused a beam misalignment, and subsequently data loss of approximately sixteen beam-days. We deeply regret this error, and wish to express our condolences.

All the very best with your assignment on Nordenmark.

Tears dripped off my nose as I read it over and over and over.

That was it. Earth had no answer for me.

Eva's head peeked through the door. "You alright?"

"It's gone." I laughed, the noise hollow and strange, and wiped my cheeks. "They sent four sentences to say that sixteen days of my brain structure was lost in transfer. Three, actually, one is a closing farewell."

She flew to the terminal to read the message, brows furrowed with the effort of scouring the text for some solution. There was none to be found.

"How could they let this happen? *Sixteen* days? Sixteen. I...they just...they can't just lose someone's..." She gaped and stuttered, grappling with Earth's answer, until at last she sank into the chair next to me, face anguished. "Gods, Inga. I'm sorry. I am so, so sorry."

I nodded.

We sat in silence.

It was me who broke it.

"Was your kid alright?"

"Søren? Yeah. He's with my brother for the night, he just has nightmares sometimes." She gave a brief smile. "Who doesn't, in this place."

"Should we go through the rest of what Earth sent?" I asked.

"If you need some time to process this first, I completely underst—"

"No." I cut her off, wiping my nose on the back of my hand and straightening, opening the next file, a document on setting up satellite imaging to help calculate the dwindling Nordenmark fauna. "Beam-transfer was bound to have a mistake at some point. I knew the risk."

"Inga, we really don't have to—"

"What else should I do. No one here has known me more than a month. The data is gone." I cut her off again, staring into her big eyes, watching her sympathetic pain ebb away. Finally, she nodded.

"Okay." Eva pointed to the imaging specifications on the terminal interface. "Petter Rosenblad out at the Communications Array can help you with satellite scheduling."

We went through the documents, information on ecological collapse models filling in some dry, functional part of my artificial brain. But not the part that mattered. The absence clung, pulling at the fading light of the Canadian sun, my half-memories of boxes and ashes and desert sand.closed the door together on the carcass, tears streaming from my eyes. The sound of mechanical grinding came from beyond the walls and a glass panel above the door illuminated orange, the letters of the word DIGESTION swimming in my tears.

The room warmed as chemical reactions began dismantling the deer, heat wavering off the metal face of the door. We stood at the door until the grinding slowed to a stop. I waited until Amit gave a little nod and turned off the gas burner.

The silence in the corridor on the way back to the airlock amplified the pounding in my head until I couldn't bear it.

"I read that my body on Earth went into a digester. After I was encoded for transfer."

I heard Amit's head snap towards me, but he said nothing.

"Anyway, there's only here for me now. I hope, for all our sakes, that wasn't the last deer in Godhavn."

6

It was late when I walked out of the medical station, alone. I had agreed to let Eva run a deep scan of my brain, but wasn't expecting her to find hundreds of microscopic dead spots, inaccessible neurocels shutting down, stuck waiting for molecular information that never came. Out of range of Eva's concern I sent a ping to Amit, asking if he knew anywhere to get a drink in Godhavn. He responded right away, telling me to meet him at a place called Mass.

The assistant led me through the streets to an industrial road where two massive silos towered over the dark warehouses and detritus rolled listlessly in the dirt. At the corner of a dark alley, I spotted the name over a door. A woman leaned against the brick beneath it, smoking from a vapourizer. The scent of cloves billowed up into the warm air from her mouth as I walked up, her dark eyes following me into the bar.

The fog had found its way inside, into the shafts of light illuminating the room. It was almost empty, a handful of people scattered across the black velvet chairs, in furtive conversations or heavy silence. The woman from outside slipped in the door behind me, the clove-smoke clinging in her long hair. She clamped a hand on my shoulder and flashed a wicked smile, pulling me in towards the gleaming ebony bar top.

"So, do you like death?"

"What?" I stuttered. She pushed me down onto a stool and continued around the bar.

"Nobody comes out here unless they're transfixed by circling the drain. What do you want to drink?"

I scanned the bottles of dark botanical liquors behind her. None of them were familiar at all. "Something strong."

"Mm, you're in the right place for forgetting." She winked at me and poured a deep red syrup into two glasses. Handing one to me, she clinked the other against it and drank, hissing afterwards like a snake.

I downed mine as well, finding the taste of a bitter herb and licorice in my mouth. The burn of the alcohol was welcome, different from the aching absence, the black hole in my head. "Thanks."

The woman grinned and drew closer, black eyes burning. Up close, I could see her earrings had tiny preserved embryos dangling from them.

"So tell me, what are you here to forget about?"

"I'm here to meet someone," I said, levelly. "Amit Sandhu."

"The veterinarian. Yes, I know him well." She smiled conspiratorially, long black fingernails clinking on my glass as she refilled it. "He holds on to much that should be forgotten."

"Maybe," I said.

Her eyes flicked up over my shoulder. "Speak of the devil."

Amit slid onto the stool next to me. The circles under his eyes looked as if they were carved in stone. "Hi Inga. I see you've met Kali."

"Amit, my shepherd, it's good to see you." Her smile widened, and she came around the bar to tousle his hair and lick his cheek with a pointed tongue. With her arms wound around him, she turned her attention back to me.

"So you are Inga." She tasted my name, licking the vowels just as she had Amit. "A cyborg come from Earth. Your name could be translated as no one, nothingness. The absence of. I like that very much. Excuse me."

She left the bottle on the bar between us and walked off to two well-groomed men who were standing to leave. I downed a second glass.

"Isn't Kali the Egyptian goddess of fire?"

"Hindu, goddess of time, destruction, and death. It's not her real name, but it may as well be," Amit said, his expression turning urgent. "Did you get the response from Earth?"

He watched me pour and drink a third glass.

"Yeah."

"...And?"

Where to start. "They didn't send much. Some routines for satellite assistance, schematics for elderly care drones, a planning document for reducing the human population to terraforming limits again."

He shot back the scarlet liquor. "Nothing about animal welfare. Breeding programs. Recommendations on reintroducing species? Godhavn will die back to the barren rocks it came from."

I emptied my glass again, let the licorice fill my mouth. Amit's head slid down until his forehead rested on the bar. A flush rose in my cheeks while we sat in silence. One of the men with Kali had broken into tears, the other comforting him. Both men kissed Kali's hand and left. "You know, on Risha they use machines to support environmental stability."

"No, Nordenmark was designed for ecological homeostasis. The terraforming here wasn't done like on Risha, the planet's composition isn't right for that." Amit's head suddenly lifted. "Oh, Inga, I'll have fifty, sixty years of this, you're looking at what, five hundred?"

I laughed. "No, don't worry. They beamed part of my brain off into a pulsar, so I doubt I have that long anymore." The words were so easy to say through the buzz.

"What?" Amit stared. "They did what?"

"Sixteen beam-days' worth of my brain just sailed off into the void of space. Beam misalignment. All those memories…" I whistled, casting my hand to the side.

"Ah. Shit." He winced and downed his glass. I refilled it.

Both of us jumped as Kali's fist slammed down on the bar.

Her eyes sparked, but her smile returned in a flash. "Amit. None of this misery. She came here to forget."

Amit rested his chin on his hands. "There's no help coming, no ship of embryos being sent out. Earth is letting Nordenmark go, Kali. This is it, this is the end."

I jumped as a glass smashed on the wall behind us. Kali's face was painted with fury. "Then we cut the umbilical and look our death in its face." She was terrifying, flinging the red syrup from her talons as she roared. "The ego of you scientists, thinking yourself gods. You can't hold back death. This universe ends in silence."

I reeled as if she had slapped me, but Amit weathered her words unmoved, shaking his head.

"You don't have to watch it die."

"I have had to watch it plenty." Kali spat, "Our difference is that I know what I control and what I do not." When Amit didn't respond, she tossed her hair and stormed off. I watched her go, touching the drops of liquor spattered across the bar top, soaking in her heady certainty.

"She's right, Amit." I murmured, "Nothing we do now will change anything. The funeral rhyme you gave me even says it—*all our days will end like this.*"

Amit laughed a little, rubbing his face. "Ah, I know. I know she's right, I would be better off accepting the collapse. I just... Maybe fighting it won't change the outcome, but I *can't* give up on them. I can't do nothing."

I thought of the little beam-fragments of my life, my brain, careening away from the rest of me with every second. The depolarizer that kept me here to unravel in their absence. "If there's no bringing it back, anything you do or don't do amounts to nothing."

He shook his head, face dark in anger, but said nothing. When his drink was finished, Amit rose to leave, mumbling about being on call in the morning.

I let him go. The deer's funeral wasn't nothing. It wasn't. There was a twinge of guilt underneath the woozy distance of the alcohol. But I ignored it.

"Wish I could end all of this for him, break Nordenmark back into the cursed atoms it came from," Kali mused, coming up behind me as the door closed after Amit. She cocked her head, earrings swinging. "Why someone would come all the way here is baffling."

"So I hear." My drink sloshed over the side of my glass. "Things got a lot worse after I started to beam-transfer."

"They couldn't take you back?"

"I'm dead on Earth." I revelled in the surprise on her face. "Getting encoded for the beam destroys the organic brain. So I died, and then transferred through the beamline, and now I'm here. The stochastic prediction of electron states can only be done with the whole consciousness in the beam, so there's only one shot. And no one has ever transferred out of a printed brain."

"Oh, interesting." She leaned in, her gaze intense. "So, what was your purgatory like? Did you wait on the bridge? Burn in a lake of fire?"

Her interest caught me off guard. "Uh, no, there wasn't anything like that. It was just nothing. No time. No dreams, no nightmares."

"Not until you woke up here." Her eyes flashed. "Oh, but that's a cruel beginning."

I laughed and licked the red liquor off the side of the glass, the story spooling out of me. "Yeah, the collapse now is awful. They have me out there trying to find how many beavers are left, count them up. Which, there's no point, because there aren't any, they're all dead. And then I ended up with a dead spot in my brain. Don't know what was there, but the shitty weak heart they gave me stops beating without it. So, get this—they've put a depolarizer in me so I can stick around long enough to find if any of the sick little animals actually do still exist. Collect pieces of them and make a half-hearted, incomplete archive of what's left of this place. Isn't that perfect."

"Those terra-fuckers should burn for that." I frowned at the intensity on her face. A dulled part of me resented her missing that it was Nordenmark who grew the body, who should have noticed the empty neurocels before they woke me. "Nothing good comes from thinking you know better than the universe. They should leave these rocks in peace."

"No, no...I mean Nordenmark—and Risha—they're important in the preservation of life. Redundant systems, so it doesn't disappear." It was getting hard to form the words without slurring.

"Oh." Kali rolled her eyes and mimed stabbing herself in the heart. "You're just like the shepherd! What makes Earth life so important? Most of this universe is quiet, dead space."

Her scorn boiled in my stomach. "Maybe I am like him. It must be easy to watch things die off and say that's the natural state of the universe."

She threw her head back and laughed, a deep throaty roar that cracked into an unnerving squeal. The scent of clove wafted over to me again as she shook her head at me. "Inga, my sweet no one, don't sit here destroying that expensive brain of yours and tell me of the sanctity of life. No more, tell me of something else. Tell me of Earth."

"Earth." My head was throbbing, my cheeks burned. It was impossible to capture anything solid about Earth without alcohol in my blood. Now my mind drifted through fragments and senses. "I don't know. I'm from the north. The sun is brighter than here. There are more people than here."

I mumbled through hazy descriptions of mountains and winter and a city with millions of people for an enraptured Kali, the room spinning around her sparking eyes, her smile a knife's edge on the ready anger stoked inside. I felt the same heat. I told her what I remembered about the desert, the gravel spreading out to meet the sky in all directions, but I couldn't describe what was in the middle of it, what held it all together. The words were missing, wiped away by the room's pulsing. Its absence was heavy, grew heavier, until I couldn't bear it, couldn't pull enough air into my lungs.

Then there were only flashes, of leaving Mass and Kali's vicious smile behind, of thunder rolling but no rain to break the heat. Trees whipping my face, something scratching at my leg. Holding someone's hand to drag them across the street, bare knees, laughing. Shouldn't have drank so much. Couldn't focus on my wearable, couldn't see where it was taking me. Running down a dark sandy hill together, the lone beautiful moon hanging in a bright crescent overhead.

Stumbling over something and coming to rest.

There was no separation between the inky forest and sky, only a darkness where insects crawled over my hands, my face. Inspecting the intruder. Shouldn't be in the forest at night, Inga. The bugs will eat you alive. It was a quiet voice that protested, a stronger one that said let go, rest.

Blackness seeped through the dark branches.

It hurt. Even though I couldn't remember what was gone, the absence hurt.

Should have left with Amit. Apologized.

A deer with its head hanging crookedly chased me through the uneasy abyss, my mind filled with screaming.

7

I rolled over and vomited into a cluster of ferns. A burning in my chest had brought me back to the dim Godhavn daylight. The sting of the depolarizer joined a cacophony of smaller pains—scratches on my skin, a dull ache behind my eyes.

I sat up, carefully, and crawled away from the ferns.

My legs had given out in the bushes at the edge of a forest lake, their failure saving me by a matter of steps from drowning. No amount of depolarization would have brought me back from that. The black depths smelled clean, welcoming, open air away from the forest crowding the beach, and so wide the opposite shore disappeared in the fog. My assistant complained that I was somewhere called Stora Björn, dehydrated and missing my dose of stabilization drugs, with the beginnings of several skin infections.

I stripped off my jumpsuit and plunged into the cool water, rinsing the sweat of revival off my body. I wanted to dive, to escape into the pressure of the water's embrace, but with these shallow lungs I didn't dare. So I floated, ears full of thuds and groans from the deep, staring up at the washed-out sky. What came next? Plagues of insects, trees covered in beetle blight. Would the fish survive, or freshwater shrimp, or crabs. Would anything survive. Maybe I would just float here until my heart stopped again.

No.

I had promised.

I had promised her that I'd come back soon.

The guilt of leaving Hecate alone dragged me back to shore.

As I walked along the beach, the pain started again and I began to cry, shuddering sobs that threatened to split apart my ribs, crack my chest open. It hurt, and this was how it was now. If it took nine days for the beam to reach Nordenmark from Earth, those memories were at the edge of the universe by now. I would never know what was gone.

My stomach churned, a sickly vortex bubbling up around my heart. I willed the world to stop spinning, resisting yet another depolarization. I hadn't brought any of the stabilization medication with me. It was a long way back to the apartment and my head ached, a thick paste of thoughts coating it. My boot tangled on a patch of stinging plants and I stumbled into them, sinking to my knees. The flickering images of ashes and boxes and dead empty desert returned, unbidden. I longed for the dark, cool peace of the water.

No, if I lay down here, she would be all alone.

Grasses clutched at my feet as I made my way to the tram, vines sewing themselves over my path, but I kept going. Halfway to the station I vomited again, slippery bile coating the back of my nose, the sides of my teeth, but at last my feet shuffled onto the platform.

The window of the tram reflected a gaunt, sunken human speckled with light-yellow beetles. My hair crawled with life. Exhausted faces met me inside the warm tram car, repulsed stares touching me, though only for a moment. I sat down next to an indolent woman in a limp green dress who leaned her head against the window, strands of greying hair escaping in a halo. Her eyes slid over me, and she shifted her body away from mine. I focused on her shoes as the tram rocked its way into Godhavn, on the weave and creases of the braided hessian and leather. It was a relief to walk out of the car and into the weathered city street, swallowed incrementally further by the forest since I had left it. My head swam as I climbed the stairs to my apartment.

Hecate was sitting on the kitchen counter, tongue flickering in suspicion as I swallowed a dose of stabilization chemicals and drank straight from the dehumidifier tap, gulping the tinny water until it splashed down my face. I sank to the kitchen floor, Hecate creeping forward to peek down at my sorry state. I shook my head.

"I'm sorry I didn't come home, I won't do it again. Earth lost part of my brain. I wasn't thinking."

The damask lizard blinked at me, rolling the toes of her velvety foot over the edge of the countertop. I slid onto my back on the warm floor, the yellow beetles clambering off of me and into the cracks in the old apartment. There was a soft creaking as Hecate climbed down to hunt the slow-moving insects. I closed my eyes, traced my fingers over her velvet skin.

"I'm glad that you're eating. Keep your strength up."

Some time later I awoke in darkness. The ache behind my eyes was gone, the roiling in my stomach subdued. I waved a hand over my wearable, and the light turned on. It was dark outside, and my wearable chimed that

I was due for the next dose of the stabilization drugs. I dragged myself to my feet and downed the powdery capsules.

"Hecate?"

I craned my neck, the muscles around my shoulders screaming after lying on the floor. The deadwood was empty. I bent to look under the bed, saw her dark shape curled up in the tub I had placed there for her. "There you are."

Her shadow didn't move.

"Hecate?"

I dropped to my knees, tapping gently at the tub's edge. No response. I pulled the tub out into the light.

She lay still, tail curled around itself. Eyes open. One foot resting over the green shoots I had placed there yesterday.

It was only me and the spiders in the apartment now.

"No, don't leave me," I whispered, stroking her lifeless head. "I thought we were in this together."

I sat holding her until the light dimmed and shut off. The absence inside my chest grew into devouring jaws that ate away at me, the humid quiet drew in until I gasped for air. I had to tell someone. It was the middle of the night. Amit said he was on call. The twinge of guilt at letting him go from Mass resurfaced. I sat wheezing, arguing with myself. He couldn't hold that against me. After the deer, he would understand. He knew her. There wasn't anyone else. I could sit here alone with my dead lizard until I died as well, but it would be slow, uncomfortable, with the depolarizer bringing me back as long as it could.

—*Hecate's gone.*

I croaked out the message. My finger tapped to send it.

It was terrible without her. Suffocating. With only the ticking dehumidifier fan to keep me company, the fear trickled in. I was choking on tears by the time Amit's reply came.

—*I'm so sorry. Am at ITB tonight if you want company.*

The relief was crushing.

I gulped for air as I wrapped her little body in a clean towel and placed it into the linens box. For the last time, we set out up the hill. The red city night cast a demonic glow in the thick fog, stretching the silhouettes of the buildings, turning hanging branches into claws that brushed over me. It dimmed at the cemetery, where the black tendrils of vines tore at the broken gravestones.

I held the box close and walked into the stygian forest.

The wet of dew was made slimy against my skin by the exudates of vines and trees as my eyes searched for light or shadow. I felt my way along the path until the hum of dehumidifiers emerged in the blackness, until my fingers found the handle of the front door. When I walked into the cool, dry air of the laboratory, Amit sat up from a cot.

"Gods, Inga, are you alright?"

I rubbed a hand across my tear-streaked face. As the lights turned up, I could see a dark bruise cutting a menacing arc over one of Amit's eyes, swollen shut.

"Shit, are you?" I mumbled, placing Hecate on the lab bench.

He walked over, eyeing the scratches on my face and arms. "Distillate can hit pretty hard. One of my neighbours used to be a deer hunter, his place is still covered in antler racks. I picked a fight."

"Did you win?" I asked.

"Does it look like I did? He's twice my size." Amit shook his head and gave a half-grimace, touching clumsy stitches over his brow. "Never mind. What happened with Hecate?"

"I don't know." My voice trembled no matter how deep a breath I took. "Uh...she was on the counter when I got home, she was eating. I fell asleep, I woke up...and she was gone."

"Ah." He nodded. "You know there's nothing you could have done. She was sick."

I opened the box. Her body lay inside, still vacant. Tears rolled off my nose, splashed onto her skin. I missed her presence. Amit put an arm around my thin shoulders until my tears subsided into gasping convulsions.

"I'm sorry, Amit... I know it's not rational to be sad about a single lizard dying," I croaked at last, dragging a hand across my stinging eyes.

"You lost someone you cared about." He let go of me, patting my arm. "You've lost a lot. I get it."

"Thank you," I whispered, blinking back more tears, willing my voice steady. "Does she have to be put in the digester?"

"We can wait until you're ready."

"I'm not."

He nodded.

"I have some soup."

"Soup." I repeated it dumbly, my brain unable to process the word.

"Yeah. It's my ritual, but I can lend it to you. Come on."

I followed Amit into the small kitchen bathed in eerie green light, where he pulled a container from the cooling unit and set it to heat. The sharp mix of herbs that wafted over made my stomach growl. He poured it into two small bowls and gave me one.

"Here. Meng Po's soup of oblivion."

I sipped the warm liquid, spicy and salty. "Who's Meng Po?"

"Goddess of oblivion. You haven't gotten to her in the book?"

Tears filled my eyes. "If I did, I can't remember."

"Ah. Well, she stands at the Naihe Bridge and gives this soup to the dead. They drink it before they are reincarnated, to forget the suffering of their past lives." He drank from the small bowl, then sat pushing a fallen drop around on the table surface. "The main ingredient is supposed to be all the tears cried in your lifetime, so this version is probably not very effective, but the herbs are good. And it's nice to think of forgetting this all."

I sipped from the bowl. "She hasn't been on the other side when I've been dead. Just nothing. Cold, uneasy nothing."

He touched the skin over his eyebrow again. "What do I know. Maybe there is only nothing on the other side. At this point, that might be nice."

"Amit, why do you know all these death deities?"

He stared into his soup. "I went looking for them. Before all this. I needed something to help let go of the bad cases. They have all these small rituals to help cope with the grief, and I'm connected by them to other people who went through the same thing. And then, you know, it was all bad cases, entire species going extinct. So now, anything that helps."

Extinct. The word rattled in my head. "Have you ever met Freja Ek?"

"The name sounds familiar."

"They we re part of the Skellefteå project."

Amit's eyebrows furrowed, and he winced. "No, that's a shady part of Nordenmark's history. I guess it probably laid the groundwork for bringing you here, no offence… but from what I've heard they were bending the definition of ethical science pretty hard to fuel progress. A lot of people died."

"Oh." The last herbs in the soup swirled around the bottom of my bowl. "I met Frej when I was out at Vargholmen the other day. They have these beautiful crows."

"Crows. As in the bird?" His face was incredulous.

I nodded. "You should see them. They look exactly like the real thing, only they're automatons."

His face fell a bit. "Ah. That's nice."

8

After four days of running samples to distract myself, sleeping on the cot in the lab to avoid the emptiness of my apartment, a call came in that one of the last Nordenmark otters showed up in a trap on the coastline. I trudged down the hill from the Institute, past a fresh plot at the far end of the cemetery, its wooden cross already toppled onto the soft earth by a fallen tree branch. I stopped to set it upright, throw the branch back to the forest, pull the creepers off the neighbouring graves. I felt a tiny bit better afterwards. Maybe Amit had something with his death rituals.

The second tram line took me south, the forest pocked by low housing units and stations where weeds thrust through crumbling stones and drooped from roofs. At the end of the line, I climbed onto a small transport drone and rode down an overgrown road to the Nordenmark Communications Array.

A squat stone building sat at the end of the road, an unassuming hub for integrating signals from the array spread out over the archipelago beyond the city. Parsing data beamed from Earth and Venus and Risha, and signals from the satellites above Nordenmark that tracked weather and clouds and the green creeping its way across the planet's habitable surface. I left the drone in the trampled weeds next to a leaning fence and shivered. Every part of me on Nordenmark had trickled through here and down a cable to the medical station. It was the umbilical on my way into this body.

The building's entrance opened into a dim room with long rows of blinking computation racks. A man sat silhouetted against a window, turning as I entered.

"Hello, I'm Inga Nyström, I'm here about the otter."

The man walked towards me, his posture hunched, his thinning hair a sandy brown atop a weathered face. Calculating eyes took in my hair, my face, and lingered on my neck. At last, he extended a hand.

"Welcome, Dr. Nyström. I'm Dr. Petter Rosenblad."

My eyes narrowed. "Oh, I know you. I've been trying to contact you about the satellites."

"Yes. I apologize for not getting back to you yet about the schedule, the equipment is quite busy at the moment. Do you need anything before we head down to the trap?"

The otter was more important than starting an argument about resource allocation. I mustered a smile. "No, we can go right away."

"Sure. I hope we followed the procedure correctly. The veterinarian was quite thorough when he was out here some weeks back, but none of us have any real experience dealing with wildlife." He rubbed his head and took a thin jacket down from a hook by the door. "Let's go."

I followed him outside and down a gravel path, the sound of lapping waves growing louder as the forest shrank around us, trees stunted by the rocky soil.

"When was the trap triggered?" I asked.

Petter glanced back over his shoulder. "Well, the light was already on when I got here this morning, so I don't know exactly when it happened. The last person left for the evening probably six hours before I came in, but I'm not sure if they looked at it before they went or not."

We wound around a large boulder and the sea opened out, stretching until it disappeared into the grey horizon. The closest islands of the archipelago were visible, dotted with massive metal receivers that glinted in the flat light. I stopped. It was a ruffled mimic of the Canadian desert, the blue-grey water flat and endless, the wind whipping at my hair. It was breathtaking, but absence and longing put a painful edge on it. My temple began to throb and I leaned against the rocks, trying to hold on to the feeling of beauty, revive the memory of the desert. Crystallize it so I could remember it forever.

"You coming?"

It had taken Petter a moment to realize he had continued on alone, unfazed by the view. He stood on the path below, expectant.

"Just catching my breath," I called back, still trying to kindle the brightness of the northern sun in the gloom of the shore. The ache in my head was growing; I had to let it go. I kicked at the weeds and rejoined Petter on the trail down to the water. The path ended where long fingers of rock jutted from the cliffs, massive wet boulders that had broken off the land. He pointed out at one of them.

"There. The box out there is number thirteen, that's the one that was lit up."

The edge of a wire box was just visible. "Alright, thanks."

He nodded and thrust his hands into his pockets, the wind pulling the sail of his jacket tight against his hunched frame. "Well. I'm not one for swimming, and I have a process to finish still. So you just follow the trail back up when you're done. How long will you be out here for?"

"An hour or two at most."

"Alright. I'll be gone by the time you get back, but knock on the office door and someone should be able to help if you need it."

"You don't want to see the otter?"

Petter gave a curt wince. "No thanks. The critters around here are mangy things, we do our best to avoid them. You're doing a good thing, logging them and putting them out of their misery."

I frowned at him. "Well, it's better if as many as possible survive. It helps to stabilize the Godhavn biome."

"Right. Good luck, then." Petter tapped his wearable and gave a brief wave, and his shoes crunched back up the path.

I picked my way out onto the rocks, careful on the slippery seagrass that wound from the depths up onto the dark stone. At the edge I donned gloves and reeled the wire box up, pulling with all my might to move a weight that would have been effortless for my body back on Earth.

The sickly-sweet odour coming from the box made my stomach drop.

I opened the lid.

"Shit."

The creature inside mewled pitifully, staring up at me with baleful eyes from where it lay on its side, legs twitching. It was emaciated, with a badly healed broken leg and sores around its mouth.

"Shit." I ripped a glove off and fumbled to ping Amit. "Come on, come on." The wait was excruciating, my heart pounding in my throat.

"Hi Inga."

"Amit, this otter out here is barely alive. What should I do?"

"Ah. How bad is it?"

The otter rested its head back against the side of the box. It was weak, and afraid of me. "Bad. He's malnourished, his leg looks broken, he's got sores around his mouth. Hey little guy, it's alright, I'm not going to hurt you."

There was silence from the wearable as I tried to comfort the otter.

"Is there nervous system involvement? Twitching or seizing."

"...Why."

"Do you have an isofluoronide syringe in your bag?"

Tears prickled in my throat.

"Amit, no...no I can't..."

"If his nervous system is involved, it's always the prion. Don't prolong his suffering." Amit was firm.

"It can't be the prion, he's an otter." I shot back.

"If they eat something with a high enough prion load, it happens. What else would cause neurological symptoms in Nordenmark otters?"

"If you tell me what to do to stabilize him, I can bring him to the Institute and we can see." There wasn't anything else it could be, but I still fought him.

"His leg is broken. He has neurological symptoms. What else, Inga." Amit's voice was steel.

I gritted my teeth and stared at the sea. My molars threatened to crack with strain as I begged every deity

I remembered or had forgotten to claim the creature in front of me. Someone give him passage to some land of the dead, spare him from the howling abyss on the other side.

"There is a very old Indigenous legend from where you come from, Inga. A duality of deaths. Tia, a goddess of peaceful death, and Ta'xet, a god of violent death."

The otter bleated and rolled onto its stomach. It didn't have the strength to coordinate its shaking limbs. I cursed every one of those remorseless gods for their apathy.

"There are good deaths and bad," Amit continued.

"I...can't."

"Just see if you have the isofluor first."

Tears streamed down my face as I reached into my bag. Found the small case next to salve and smart bandages. Pulled out anaesthetic and antiseptics. And two syringes covered in warning labels. I laid one on my lap. I cleared my throat and took a deep breath.

"Yeah. I have the syringe."

"Okay. Use the muscle over his haunches. Stabilize his leg with your gloved hand. You want to push it in quickly, not too deep, and inject smoothly."

I squeezed my eyes shut and took a second, shuddering breath. The gate to the abyss was under my hand.

"I'm here with you, Inga."

It was quiet, and fast. Peaceful.

After I disconnected from Amit, I screamed into the sea until I was hoarse. The rock remained unchanged, the seagrass unhearing, the salts and carbon and water molecules blind. They had witnessed millennia, they had known the atoms of this otter as they cycled through rock and water and air and into being and now out again.

I wept every tear in my body into the wind, stroked the otter's fur until the clouds began to dim. When there was nothing left, I disconnected the wire crate from the notification system, closed the lid, and dragged it up onto the shore, making my way back up the rocky cliffs.

Halfway up I had to stop to catch my breath, and sat down on a bench at a lookout point. As I leaned against the metal trash bin next to the bench, the sickly-sweet smell from the otter wafted up. I pushed the trap further up the path and sat back down, but the smell remained. I sniffed, searching behind the bench. There was nothing but grass. I lifted the lid of the trash bin.

Inside were empty tins of preserved fish and a jug of insecticide.

I stared at it. Resisted making the connection.

They *poisoned* him.

Abandoned him to suffer, alone, until the abyss claimed him.

In a cold rage, I returned to the shore in the gathering dark and dragged up the other twelve traps, pulling out handfuls of poisoned fish. When every one of them was empty I pushed them into the water and let them sink, defanged, to the bottom of the sea. When they were all dismantled, I dragged the trap with the dead otter back up to the main building and pulled at the door.

It was locked.

My blood boiled in the last of the twilight as I cleaned up their destruction and loaded it onto the drone, packaging and labelling it for digestion and disposal. At last, the drone blinked to life and began crawling off towards the Institute. It was finished. I headed back into the city in darkness. Flashes of boxes and ashes, of Hecate and traps dogged me as I walked through the streets, and the black hole inside of me ached until I thought my chest would collapse.

Under a flickering red streetlamp, my vision blurred and my body fell away, and I was lost in the fury of the shrieking, frozen abyss.

9

The tram pulled into the Vargholmen station, and the lights shut off. It was still early, the thick fog draped over the platform in a blanket from the night before.

"I still don't understand why we couldn't have met at ITB," Amit said as we walked out of the car and down the stairs.

"I don't think the crows take the tram. Come on."

Tree shadows cut through the air, straining against the star cresting the horizon. It was disorienting, turning us around twice before we found the quiet shoreline. When we followed it around to the old resting area, the benches sat empty.

"We're early," I said, hoping I hadn't forgotten when we were supposed to meet. "I think we're early."

Skepticism flashed across Amit's face. It hurt, but he was right. My brain was growing more untrustworthy each time I collapsed. It had happened twice in the last three weeks; I had come to alone and disoriented on the street returning from the Array, and then ten days later it had happened in my sleep. The roaring, cold dark siphoned off a few more memories each time I visited, although never the ones that plagued me. The abyss was hungry, but not for the poisoned otter's cries.

"I used to love being out in the woods," Amit said, brushing beetles and ants from the table we sat on. "I can't stand it now. Too quiet."

"I'm sure they'll be here soon," I mused. My ears strained to hear Frej's footsteps, my ears warping the still morning into the sound of crows. This needed to go well. I picked up a rock and drew it along the bench until Amit put a hand on my wrist.

"Hold on." He twisted, searching the sky.

A flapping noise came from overhead, and the scraping call of a crow. Another responded from further away, and small twigs and leaves showered the ground as two alighted in a nearby tree. Garmr landed heavily on the table next to us, metal talons scratching the wood. Amit's hand tightened around my wrist. At once the air was filled with the thrum of feathers, the fog dappled by dark wings. More crows landed on the ground next to the table, surrounding us, flapping and muttering and prodding each other with their sharp little beaks. At last, Freja resolved out of the fog in a thick draping sweater that was covered in burrs and spruce needles.

"Hello Inga." They took a furtive glance at Amit.

"Hi Frej, this is Amit. The veterinarian from the Institute. Amit, meet Freja. I've been working with them on the proposal."

The two inspected each other in silence, Amit with wariness, Frej with uncertainty.

"So, these are the crows you made?" Amit said at last.

"Yes." Freja's tone ranged on defiance. "They're just like the original Nordenmark corvids, or as close as I could get anyways. They run on eating insects and carrion, they spread seeds. Garmr even brings me shiny things, sometimes."

Amit held a tentative hand out to Garmr, who drew in to inspect him. A coordinated chatter went up from the gathered automaton birds.

I held my breath.

"Like the proposal said, I could create otters, beavers...deer..." Frej smiled as Garmr rubbed his head against Amit's hand.

He shook his head.

"They're machines."

My heart sank.

"They're stable." I tried to find gentle words while the otter's face burned in my mind. I had asked Freja's help the day after finding it. More of the Nordenmark fauna might die, but it wasn't going to be like that. "They look just like the extinct ones, work the same way. But they're less vulnerable. They'd support the Godhavn biome, help the wildlife recover."

A frown grew on Amit's face. "They're not real. The metal is mined from the rocks. There could be knock-on effects for the...biological species."

I saw Freja's smile fade. It was hard to keep desperation out of my voice.

"Something more dangerous than the collapse? Do you really think so?"

Amit drew his hand back from Garmr. "Nordenmark was built for ecological homeostasis. An animal made from stone is functionally different from an animal made from organic matter."

"Like I am different from you?" Frej murmured.

"Ah, that's not what I mean at all, no. You and Inga aren't hundreds of animals driven by programmed instinct."

"Please, Amit. We are going to be watching the rest of this planet die if we can't find a different way forward."

His face twisted. "Inga, the animals here have been my life. I can't sign onto something that might put them at risk—if they function the same way, then there's competition for food, for breeding grounds, for territory. I... can't."

I should have known. He had said he couldn't give up fighting for them that night at Mass. The poisoned fish in the otter traps could change his mind, I was sure of it, but I still hadn't told him. I stared into the swirling fog over the lake, avoiding his eyes. It could make him understand. It could break him completely.

"I understand your fear that more of this will disappear." Frej spoke, as I watched one of the crows pluck tufts of grass out from the sand. "I created the crows because the forest went silent. I miss what's gone. Godhavn is dying, the forest now is just weeds and bugs. This is to help it recover, keep a place alive for them to return to, and fill the spaces that are permanently lost." They met Amit's eyes straight on.

"An automated forest is not the same thing as recovery. Mechanical birds and deer and frogs aren't life, there's no symbiosis, it's still just the Nordenmark rock replacing nature. All the life lost becomes nothing," he muttered.

"Making a way for the future doesn't mean destroying the past, Amit," I said.

"Ah, but so often it has. Can you say for certain the Godhavn biome won't be forgotten in all of this?"

We had reached deadlock again. I hated disagreeing with Amit. Down the beach two crows bickered over a scrap of metal from a dismantled grill. I forced myself to turn and look him in the eye, taking a deep breath.

"It doesn't matter. I'm sending a proposal to Earth for information on using automatons to help stabilize Godhavn. I don't want to do this without you. Please, Amit."

His face was stricken. "There's so few left! Don't make it harder on them to survive. Please."

"This is to *help* them. Every person alive will be here for decades. Freja for centuries. Let the dead rest, and fight for what we still might be able to save."

He rubbed his hands over his face, started to say something a few times, but stopped. At last, he stood up from the bench and walked away, back towards the tram. As he disappeared into the fog, the flickering images of blowing ashes and the otter's bleary eyes closing ravaged my head. I shuddered. Two crows followed him in the treetops, calling, the scrape of their voices accusing. And wounded.

"I don't understand your friend," Freja said. "Maybe it's an Institute thing. In Skellefteå they were so focused on the one thing, they lost sight of everything else."

"He has a good heart," I said, still watching the fog where he had disappeared, hoping he would emerge from it again, change his mind. "Kali said it like he's trapped in the grief of all this, can't let go."

To my surprise, Frej laughed. "Well, if his world is losing these animals, and mine is creating the crows, no wonder we couldn't agree. Can any of us let go of the things our worlds are made of?"

I nodded, though a bitter response to their question floated to the surface of my mind. Between the slippery shards of Earth, Hecate, the collapse, the otter… my world here was made of death. If only I could let that go.

"Gods, I hope he'll forgive me."

Freja sat down on the bench across, pulling the sleeves of their cardigan over their hands. "He's your friend. You'll find some common ground again, I'm sure. We all want the same thing."

I smiled, clinging to Frej's surety. My wearable chimed, a ping from Eva that another response had arrived from Earth, asking me to come to the medical station as soon as I could.

"That's Eva, I should go. I'll send in the proposal while I'm there. You signed off on everything?"

"I did. Look, I know how important having Amit's support was to you." Freja chewed a fingernail. "Are you sure you want to send it in?"

"Yeah, the last species are running out of time. Whatever knowledge I brought here with me is disappearing and hasn't helped much anyways. You've been here longer than anyone else, and the calculations are sound, so I can at least get Earth to send the data to help you guide a different kind of recovery."

Freja nodded, and reached over to give me a tight hug, the burrs on their cardigan sticking to my jumpsuit. "Good luck, Inga."

———

I trudged up the driveway of the medical station and into the faint smell of disinfectant. A man and a woman in scrubs crowded into the elevator with me, their hands red from washing, faces tired and drawn. Would they support the proposal or agree with Amit? Maybe they had different problems, other priorities. I left them at the experimental floor and walked to Eva's office. Concern flitted over her face when she saw me.

"The decoding just finished. From the titles of the documents it looks like there's some information that might be relevant to your receptacle body, and then the information you requested on otter locomotion and vertebrate behavioural algorithms a few weeks back."

"That's great." I managed a weak smile for her. "I need to send the proposal for building the automatons to them. Frej has signed everything."

"Oh, Søren will be excited to hear that there might be deer in the forest again," Eva remarked as she opened the first document.

"Søren from the clinical team?"

"No, Søren is my son, remember?" She smiled, the skin around her eyes crinkling. How many times had she told me about him? "We saw a deer together once when we went out to the sea, when he was small. He has a little virtual herd of them, can tell you all about what they eat and what to do if you see one. There's so little good news these days..." She tapped a small window at the bottom of the terminal and a kid with her same eyes filled the screen, face scrunched up in a smile. It felt like the first time I was seeing him.

"How old is he?"

"Eight. He says he wants to be a terraforming analyst when he's older. He's smart, he'll make it." The last words were fierce, painting him a defiant future. "Anyways, that's exciting. Did Dr. Sandhu agree to collaborate?"

"No. He isn't able to."

She nodded, and opened the files from Earth; new research trials on stabilization chemistries, recommendations for stalling memory loss in the elderly, on a fringe case of motor neuron degeneration in a beam-transferred dog. Eva looked through the communiques with interest, humming over small molecule inhibitors and electrical treatments that might stop the erosion of my artificial brain. None of it seemed applicable. I stared out the window. The twelve other beam-transferred human brains had arrived in perfect working condition.

"...I don't understand what this is though, do you?" Eva was saying.

"Hmm?" I looked back to the terminal screen, to an image of a vast stony desert fading into sporadic dark mountains, the steep shale of their peaks lit by brilliant sun. The pain was overwhelming. Tore Nyström, it said at the bottom of the image. I recognized it all, but none of the feelings, sensations, or memories of having been there came with it. As if someone else had told me stories of this place. I gasped and blew my breath out slowly, trying to force my heart rate back down.

"Inga? Are you alright?"

Eva took my pulse as I held a shaking hand over my face. The absence pulled on me, the frayed edges of the holes in my head unravelling. It all hurt so much.

"It's a place called Jasper, near where I lived on Earth. In the mountains."

"Did something happen there?"

Erratic heartbeats banged on my ribs. I writhed. "I don't know. I can't remember."

Breath came like knives in my throat.

This was it, this was the end.

"Come on, stay with me, Inga." Eva helped me slide onto the floor, pulled my feet up to rest above me.

"I can't remember. There's nothing there." I choked, tears streaming from the corners of my eyes. "I can't remember."

Eva gripped my hand, stroking my hair with the other. Her eyes were frantic, terrified. She couldn't help me. "I know, Inga, I know it's gone. Just stay with me. We'll figure this out, we'll find some way to make this stop."

Darkness pulsed at the edges of my vision as I felt Eva crawling around me, still holding tight to my hand. There was a blip from a monitor connecting. The abyss leapt, rearing to swallow me, and I slipped away, the roaring loud as I fell.

The dark was cold and angry, but there was a presence in it, drawing nearer.

I could feel it in the frozen weightlessness, detached from form and sensation, stirring in the stillness. An energy that watched me, its wavelengths flickering. Like a tongue over air.

I recognized it.

Hecate.

She had found me in the shapeless void of death.

As I struggled against the dumb confines of vacuum another facet resolved, a playful energy that brought peace to my suffocating mind.

In the howling scream of nothingness, they knew I was here, knew me. I reached out to hold them close, warm them from the cold.

10

The electric bubbling inside my chest was familiar, as was the woman holding an aeration mask over my face. There was no energy to scream, or move. Everything hurt.

"Almost thought we had lost you for good." She smiled, catlike eyes crinkling.

I was cold, soaked with sweat. People bustled in the room around me. I closed my eyes.

"Inga, do you know where you are?"

"Edmonton, Canada." The words were an effort.

"Do you know what happened?"

I dragged a hand over myself, resting my fingers over the implant in my chest. "Depolarizer."

"Do you remember what happened just before?"

"She was there." My eyelids fluttered, the halo of an overhead light contorting above me. "She found me."

A hand squeezed mine. "Inga? Who are you talking about?"

"Hecate," I murmured.

There was a long silence, and a tingling that spread up my arm. I shuddered, the sounds of the monitor and instruments becoming louder. The bed was uncomfortable under the protruding bones of my body, the sting of a needle hurt my hand.

"Inga? Are you with me? Do you know who I am?"

I opened my eyes, searched for a name for her face. "I think so."

Her cat eyes flicked back and forth over me. "Who's Hecate?"

The exudate of death swam through my brain, taking down circuits, spawning black holes. "She lives in my apartment."

Her eyes moved away to someone else. "Up the drip speed. Inga, do you remember what happened just before you passed out?"

A flash of desert sky burned through my head, moths crawling under hot August shale. A familiar voice telling me about extinct bears. We did everything together since his parents moved in down the street when we were six years old. There was a clicking noise. My teeth chattered. "They sent a picture. Of Jasper."

"Her temperature's low." A man's voice brought a warm blanket.

"Do you remember anything about Jasper?" The woman's voice transformed the sound of its name.

"The sun was hot in the summer..." I whispered. The clicking noise came again.

"There it is again, the activity spike," the man's voice said.

"Massive accelerans input from the brain. Shit, no wonder her heart's been crashing."

The room hummed, tendrils of pulsing darkness seeping under my eyelids. I felt the warmth of the sun again. The crunch of the gravel under my feet. And the presence that I had longed to feel for years. I turned and Tore was there, a spade in his hands, a dead blue jay at his feet. Brilliant blue as the sky. He survived. He had escaped the black holes.

"We should bury it. Lay it to rest," he said. His face looked so sad. My heart was being shredded into a million pieces.

"I don't want to go to another funeral," I murmured.

"Shit, it's spiking again. Kristoffer, depolarize her before it kills her!"

The words clouded Tore's face, erasing his eyes, the side of his jaw. He was slipping away again, like the desert gravel off the tip of his spade, like when the cancer burrowed through his brain and took him from me.

I reached out for Tore. "No, don't leave me again."

"I'm right here with you, Inga, stay with me."

We laid the blue jay's body into a shallow grave with our six-year-old hands and filled it in.

"Now, Eva!"

My vision filled with brilliant white pain, snakes of light searing the desert, the rocks, the sun, the sky burnt to a crisp.

I screamed as the memory of Tore burnt away, as my heart shuddered and died with him all over again, as he turned back into the tiny cardboard box of ashes they gave me. My whole world as ashes, blowing away in the desert wind. Until they were gone, and I was alone.

The woman named Eva had ugly sets of fingernail gashes in front of her ear, red spotted lines from my hands tearing at her, but she looked at me with pity. Not fear.

"You fought like we were trying to kill you," she said.

"They could hear you screaming on the first floor, even with the sedative," the man named Kristoffer added. His arms were coated in fresh bruises, an angry burgundy.

"I'm so sorry," I said, tears filling my eyes. "I remember lying on the floor next to the terminal, and then just…pain." A wave of nausea welled up at the memory of it.

"It's alright. Try not to beat yourself up about it." Kristoffer waved it off from where he sat working on the depolarizer outside my chest.

"It did let us figure out what's been causing your heart problems," Eva said.

I wiped a tear off my face. "Does this mean I'm free of the depolarizer?"

They exchanged a glance.

"Yes and no," Eva said. "You've been getting a massive electrical buildup in your accelerans circuit that gets discharged all at once, stopping your heart. And Kristoffer thinks we could prevent this from happening…if you depolarize regularly."

"Oh." Whatever drugs they had given me were wearing off, I could feel the gnawing inside of my chest again.

"You'll be able to at least choose a more convenient time for it," Kristoffer added, sliding a shaded glass over his eyes while he altered some part of the tiny machine. "And if you keep the charge low, it shouldn't build up to the point where it's causing electrical damage in your brain anymore."

"This should stop it from getting worse," Eva said, squeezing my hand. "You might not quite live a millennium, but you'll outlive Søren."

I nodded, even though I didn't know who Søren was.

Kristoffer brought the depolarizer to me, the wires of the device hanging over the edge of his gloved hand.

"I've modified this to notify your wearable when it detects accumulating charge."

"We just need your consent to proceed with this." Eva gave an encouraging smile. "You'll be back to your proposal for supporting the Nordenmark fauna in no time."

Their expectant faces grew puzzled at my tears. The painful absence that had haunted me since I had come to on this planet was still there, shrouded. Unknown. A hole inside of me that ached with longing. It couldn't be fixed. It would be there in every waking moment.

No.

I had promised Freja.

I didn't want them to be alone if everything was lost on this little planet.

"You can proceed."

The two physicians bustled to life, and soon the thick ooze of sedation crawled through me again, stemming my tears, lulling me with artificial presence.

11

Droplets of warm rain splattered against my head as I sat in the cemetery. The sound was different against the printed filament than it had been on my bone skull. It had taken a week to stabilize my condition in the medical station, and in that time, weeds had sprung up thick around the graves. I had finished cutting them back, slowed by lingering weakness, chasing the spiders and beetles back into the forest. One of Freja's crows sat on the grave of the unnamed infant of the Bengtsson family, gleaming midnight blue. The fan of her tail was notched on one side.

I had taken to calling her Tia. I didn't know why, but there was a warm familiarity in that name.

"You can tell I'm stalling, can't you."

Her eye glittered at me, and she flew up to a branch hanging over the entrance of the path to the Institute. I sighed and stood to follow her.

"Maybe he's forgiven me."

Swarmed with fish flies, Tia flying overhead, I climbed through the forest to the Institute. She was waiting on the roof of the building's entrance when I emerged. Amit was just a few meters away now. I had put this off long enough.

The laboratory was dark, and smelled like rot and blood. When my eyes adjusted, I saw Amit sitting on the floor with a large grey hare and an IV unit. The animal's patchy fur had come off in sheaves around where it lay, head flattened against Amit's knee. The IV unit had been shut off. The hare lay still.

"You're alive." His words were short, flat.

"Partially, at least. Who's this?"

"The last male snowshoe hare. Someone found it roaming the city. Got hit by a drone." He heaved a sigh, cradling the animal.

I sat down and nudged him very gently with my shoulder. "You alright?"

"He's long gone. I tried to save him. But it was bad." Amit's jaw twitched. "None of those gods exist. You were right, there's nothing at the end. We are all alone."

He took a shuddering breath and blew it out, blinking up at the ceiling. I nudged him again with my shoulder and let him lean back on me. There were no words that could touch the pain of absence.

"You were right to send the proposal for automatons without me." His voice broke. "I can't let go."

"I know."

There was a long pause.

"You've been sitting here for a while."

Amit nodded. "I should have moved him to the digester. I just...I can't..."

"It's alright. I can." I squeezed Amit's shoulder and crawled over to lift the hare from his lap, set it on the bench. This part I remembered. I dug a burner out from a drawer and lit it, found a vial of white paint to make the wayfinder over the hare's heart, and wrapped its mangled body up in a warm, clean towel. Amit sat staring into space through red-rimmed eyes. When it was done, I bent over its velvet ears and whispered, "I will find you in the abyss."

When I returned from the digester, Amit had his head buried between his arms. He looked up, wiping his nose on the back of his hand. "Is it done?"

I nodded.

He rested his head against the wall. "How am I supposed to be in a world without them?"

I thought for a moment. "Freja could make you a hare automaton."

Amit sniffed and shook his head. "Hares are a prey species. There's no point to a hare in an automated fauna."

"Some people might say there's no point in holding a funeral for a deer," I said gently. "It could be a memorial. An animated memory of the species. Something to hold onto in their absence."

"It's not the same."

"It's not supposed to be. A memorial doesn't replace something." I held my hands out to him, and after a moment he took them.

Hand in hand, we walked down the hill in the fog, Tia following in the clouds overhead. We walked through the cemetery, into the city where stone and metal and processed wood struggled against the encroaching wild green.

―――――

Once out of the tram station at Vargholmen, the wet forest reclaimed us, the dark trees laden with rain. We heard Freja's presence before we saw them, Tia's calls answered with beating wings and croaking multiplied from many beaks and bodies, dark shapes rustling in the trees overhead. Frej was sitting at the edge of one of the wooden tables, a tool kit spread out under a spotted umbrella. They smiled as we approached.

"Hey. I was just about to leave, it's getting dark."

"You've been busy," I said.

"There's twenty of them now." Their smile widened, then faded as they took in Amit, pants stained with the hare's blood, his eyes hollow. I squeezed his hand, but his face remained blank.

"Can I ask a favour?" I asked.

"Shoot."

"Could you create something like a hare, or a rabbit?"

"They're a prey species, we didn't put them on the list." Freja's eyes darted between Amit's slumped posture and me. "But…their body plan is probably not that different from the small mammal prototype I've been working on. It wouldn't be impossible. Bigger legs, bigger ears. But why a hare?"

"The last male snowshoe hare just died." Amit's voice was lifeless.

"Oh. I'm sorry."

"I told Inga there wasn't any purpose for an automaton hare."

"Well, we're not constrained by evolution. It could have a different purpose," I said. "Species enumeration, maybe. Or it could spread pellets of chaperonin granules to decontaminate prion residue. Make it safe for future sheep and deer."

Amit shook his head. "Why. They're gone too."

"The point is memory." Frej's words were matter-of-fact. "Only the oldest generations here grew up with crows in the sky. If things keep deteriorating, soon no one is going to remember a life with birdsong. No one here will remember Godhavn."

"Ah." Amit gave a weak shrug.

"You're too young to know." Freja stood up, scooping tiny gears and screws and drills back into the tool kit and tucking a motionless crow with one wing under their arm. "Come to my house. I'll show you." They tapped their shoulder and whistled, and the largest black bird flapped down from the tree to roost there. "Time to go, Garmr."

We followed Frej down a narrow path in the encroaching dusk to where the woods thinned and the path opened out onto a side road, abandoned and crumbling. A single red streetlamp stood at the far end, lighting remnants of fencing held up by the thick bushes grown through them. Just before the first houses of Vargholmen, Freja turned and led us to a domed warehouse with double doors. Piles of scrap sat in the yard around it, clusters of wires and metal around a massive standing antenna.

"Come on in," Frej said over their shoulder. "It'll just take me a sec to find this."

They wrenched open the doors, hinges squealing, and we walked through a boxy entrance into the main room. My mouth dropped open.

Garmr fluttered up to roost under the half of the ceiling painted deep blue, the Nordenmark constellation picked out across it in white. As the dome rose and fell, the colour morphed until it became lightest blue on the other side, streaked by wispy cirrus clouds. A raised platform running halfway around the circumference was furnished as a house, with a sofa and terminal and small kitchenette. But the main floor was magical, covered in the chaos of creation; pictures and drawings of hummingbirds and penguins, piles of tiny motors and batteries, models of feathers and wings dancing on wires. At the center of it all, a flickering light projection showed a heron in endless flight over a vast sunny sea. Amit drew towards it, transfixed, watching its feathers ruffle as it banked in an updraft above little whitecap waves.

"Freja, this is incredible," I said.

They stopped sorting through a box and ran a hand over their smooth head, nose wrinkling. "You're kidding, right? It's such a mess. I was trying to work out a soaring circuit to get some better energy use during longer flights."

Amit pointed to the projection. "Is this from Earth? I've never seen a bird like this."

"Yeah." I nodded. "It's a heron."

"It's beautiful."

"They went extinct, a long time ago. Habitat loss and the plastic in their bellies."

"Ah." Amit looked shaken.

"Here, here it is." Frej crouched next to the squat projector's lens and plugged a storage drive into it. The heron winked out, and was replaced by the familiar white clouds of Nordenmark. The projection panned down over the trimmed skyline of a younger Godhavn, over which dots flew back and forth, the air filled with trills and chirps. It cut to a field, a group of three snowshoe hares munching on plants, a doe and her fawn strolling through the background. It looked like old films from the base of the mountains in Canada, before the desert reached it. It made my heart ache.

"What is this," Amit whispered.

"It's Vargholmen, about a hundred and twenty years ago. Before the collapse," Freja said, pointing to different parts of the projection. "These deer were part of a herd that my parents were building up when it was new grassland out here. I miss all the birds, I've even forgotten how loud they were."

"There were so many of them." Amit blinked. "They're all gone."

I put my arm around his shoulders. "I know it's not the same as the hares surviving, Amit. But don't lose the memory of what they were and why they were important here." I gave him a gentle squeeze, as the image of a swell of ashes falling over a blue jay flashed in my head, the ever-present absence tearing at my heart.

Freja rolled back to the projection of the three hares, and after a long moment, Amit nodded.

12

As I got off the tram that night, I heard the faint chiming begin, the signal that my artificial brain was holding too much charge and I needed to depolarize. The apartment registered my heartbeat and the light from the bathroom turned on, a faint amber spilling over the bed. The room still felt hollow, quiet except for the curtains shifting against Hecate's deadwood. I sat down, watched a centipede make its way through the patch of light.

The chiming continued.

I sat there for over an hour.

I sat there until I was afraid of what I'd lose if I put it off any longer.

I tapped my wearable, found the program Kristoffer had installed. I lay back on the bed, pressing my hand over the depolarization implant, taking slow, even breaths.

"The dark, quiet abyss…" I murmured.

The wearable chimed.

I tapped it to confirm.

A jolt flooded my chest, like lightning striking close by, filling my ears and mouth with darkness, erasing my body.

The abyss roared, cold and vast, but it wasn't empty.

Hecate flickered in the void, the light of a pulsing star. The playful presence was with her again. The otter, at peace. And in their constellation was another, the last of his kind, gratefully at rest.

It is good to see you at peace, I thought.

The constellations of the Nordenmark dead looked back at me, quieting. All the lights extinguished from the forest surrounded me here in the abyss, cold but silent.

I took them all in my arms and held them.

You are not alone, I breathed.

———————

The electric foaming was inside my chest, my voice croaking as I gasped. A small moth fluttered against the naked lamp.

I checked my wearable.

I had been dead for less than thirty seconds.

Godhavn outside was dark, the red of the street lamps fighting with the light from the bathroom on the wood floor as I paced it. The imprint on the bed where I had died watched me circle the room, checking my memory against the wearable's data. I had just come from Freja's house. The last snowshoe hare had died earlier.

My memories were intact.

That did nothing to calm the restlessness.

I didn't want to talk with Frej, or Amit, or Eva. I needed someone who knew death, and who wasn't afraid of it. I opened the door of the apartment to free my pacing feet, and found myself at the door to Mass.

The bar was empty, save for Kali behind the counter. She looked up from a deck of tarot cards she had spread across the shining black surface, and a smile grew across her blood-red lips. I came in and sank onto a stool.

"Inga, my wandering soul, my no one. Welcome in. Amit is at home safe and asleep. You brought him peace today."

She peered into my face, then reached across to cup my cheek in her ringed hand, wiping something from underneath my eye with her thumb.

"I'm glad," I said.

She got up to pour me a steaming mug of tea, the herbs sharp. I breathed it in.

"You look like death," she said.

"I was dead, about an hour ago."

She leaned her elbows on the countertop, the smell of clove wafting towards me. "How was the abyss today?"

"Full. Empty. Loud. Quiet." I shook my head. "I don't know. Familiar and strange."

"Tell that to my father, if you find him there." She was amused. "He would like your contradictions."

"I wouldn't know where to look for him. It's a terrible, angry nothingness."

"Sounds right for Nordenmark's dead. Tilling inert land, the livestock wasting away, the collapse of the eco-system. Pestilence, famine, death. Old-world terrors."

"None of the old-world gods," I said.

"Ahh, my Inga." She took my hands and warmed them between hers, looking into my eyes. "I am grateful you bring calm to the abyss, that our dead are held by someone who understands the unbearable lightness of losing their world. They have been so alone."

I stared back at her. Her eyes burned with a dark fire, but within it I saw the same absence that was gnawing inside of me. The unbearable lightness of losing one's world. I nodded. Her understanding took an edge off the pain.

"Thanks, Kali."

"Mm." Kali sighed, releasing my hands and pulling another card from the deck. She grinned as she set it in front of me, a skull with a white flower in its mouth against a brilliant sunrise.

"Drink your tea, Inga. Death is hard on a body."

13

Three months or so after I found myself at Mass, Amit and I stood in Frej's domed warehouse as they brought the hare to life. It had turned out perfect: round and soft, with mottled brown fur and a white tail. Freja tightened a screw and it leapt up with a kick, bounding on enormous back legs to hide under the bench beside me.

"It's alright, you're alright," I told him as he cowered, eyes wild. As my hand came nearer, he leaped out and ran away.

"Maybe his fear circuitry is too sensitive," Frej said, making a shushing noise, but as they drew nearer the hare juked and headed towards Amit.

In one smooth motion, Amit dropped a towel over it and scooped it up, one hand wrapped around its hind legs, the other under its stomach. It quieted as he murmured to it, long ears resting flat as he carried the automaton out into the yard.

"No, I think you did it right. Don't want him to be too tame." I followed Freja outside behind Amit, biting my tongue as the otter flashed into my head. "You have a name for him?"

Amit set the hare down, its nose twitching to smell through the Godhavn fog. "I thought maybe *Lepus autonomicus.*"

"A new species. I like that." Freja nodded.

The hare took a tentative hop towards the trees, and Amit turned to us. "What function did you give him?"

"Two. His energy comes from eating back the grass." Frej said, "But his ecological function is to scan for animals and send their stats to Inga. So, he's like a sentinel for the living fauna."

The hare hopped closer to the forest, and in a few moments had disappeared.

"I hope it works," Amit said. "I mean, I am recommending intensive monitoring to make sure every release from your project doesn't affect the extant species. But...thank you." Freja's mouth crooked in a delighted smile, and they reached out to give him a quick hug.

"We'll try to do right by them, Amit. We have Earth's historical conservation programs and their outcomes to guide us. Hopefully..." I faltered. The word was tenuous and fragile in the still air.

"Hopefully, in a year or two things will look better here," Frej finished for me. They nodded emphatically, surveying the edge of the trees.

Amit gave me a brief smile. It was a big hope for a silent forest. I was holding on to what Kali said, describing my journey here as one of peace. Holding the Nordenmark dead, preserving their memory, if not helping to find their salvation.

Every part of me felt the gravity of that task.

The next day Freja, Amit, and I travelled out beyond Vargholmen, past the abandoned farmhouses with walls fractured by the roots of climbing vines, past the copses of new trees, out to the pioneer edge of Godhavn. We passed etched stones, their runes marking where blades of new grass had struggled out to claim another piece of rocky soil in decades past. These fell away long before we found the place where lichens and invisible microorganisms explored the land, forging ahead in green streaks where they took a new foothold, falling back where the inert rock prevailed. It was quiet here at the border of life, Amit and Frej's voices hushed as they discussed the behavioural patterns and territorial range of caribou. I'd found an old relationship between the extinct tundra cervids and the forage lichens they ate, delicate tangles of tiny branches that broke rocks into soil and prions into amino acids. Amit was going to sample the fungi here, Freja to design a wandering stag with magnificent antlers. I wanted to see the edge. No one had been out here in years, though the green margins still crept outwards, unattended. I left the others, walking onto the bare rocks that stretched out to touch the low-hanging cloud, melding with the fog, listening to the respiration of this world. For now, it breathed.

Part of me wanted to stay right there, monitoring for any hint of a change in the weak but steady rhythm, but I knew that soon the soft chime of my wearable would begin again and I would leave Frej and Amit to travel into Godhavn, back to the apartment where it all began.

I would lie on the bed, as I would for decades to come, and run the program in my wearable. Press one hand to the depolarization implant.

With a jolt, another death would take me, and I would find the abyss, frozen and roaring.

It would quiet, as I would gather them to me.

And hold the grieving dead of Nordenmark.

ACKNOWLEDGMENTS

Thanks to:

The excellent humans at Psychopomp for wanting to read about goths in space, which was the seed from which this story grew. You've made this journey of publishing a fantastic one. Long live the indie press.

Nicasio Reed for being an incredible editor to work with. Thank you for every one of your excited comments, and for every one that challenged me to write the strongest version of this story I could.

Laura Blackwell for teaching me about commas, grammar, and advances in post-mortem science.

MMIX (Rust MacCarthy and L. Faunt) for the cover art.

The Stockholm Writers Group for critique and unwavering support. The Edinburgh Science

Fiction and Fantasy folks for generously sharing morale, support, and advice with this interloper.

Everyone back home who was with me at the vet college, the anatomy department, and especially at The Underground.

And to Henrik, for helping me get this far.

www.ingramcontent.com/pod-product-compliance
Lightning Source LLC
Chambersburg PA
CBHW030010010826
48973CB00009B/2739